DOUBLE NEGATIVE

DOUBLE NEGATIVE

Ivan Vladislavić

Introduced by Teju Cole

LONDON · NEW YORK

First published in 2010 by Umuzi, an imprint of Random House Struik
This edition first published in 2013 by And Other Stories

www.andotherstories.org
London – New York

ISBN 9781908276261
eBook ISBN 9781908276278

A catalogue record for this book is available from the British Library.

Typesetter: Tetragon, London; Typefaces: Linotype Swift Neue and Verlag;
Printed and bound by the CPI Group (UK) Ltd, Croydon, CRO 4YY.

CONTENTS

for
Alan and Denise Schlesinger
and for
Felicity and Mark Murray

INTRODUCTION

Saul Auerbach, the great fictional photographer at the heart of Ivan Vladislavić's *Double Negative*, is more meticulous than most. The unhurried processes and careful results of his photography, taken on the streets and in the homes of the people of Johannesburg, provide the calm pulse of the novel. Photography is a fast art now, except for those who are too old-fashioned to shoot digital. But for most of the art's history – until about fifteen years ago – most photographers had no choice but to be slow. Film had to be loaded into a camera, the shot had to be taken with some awareness of the cost of materials, the negative had to be developed and the print had to be enlarged. A certain meticulousness was necessary for photographs; a certain irreducible calmness.

The narrator of *Double Negative* is Neville Lister, 'Nev' to his friends and family, a smart young college dropout when we first meet him. He is anything but calm. Nev's life, detailed in a discontinuous narrative from his youth to his middle age, is the main material of the novel, but it

unfurls to the steady rhythm of Auerbach's photographs:
Nev anticipating the photographs, witnessing the places
and persons involved in their making, remembering the
images years later, and remembering them years later
still. Like every worthwhile first-person narrator, Nev has
a suggestive and imprecise identification with his author.
Meanwhile, the fictional Saul Auerbach has a real-life cog-
nate in David Goldblatt, the celebrated photographer of
ordinary life in South Africa for the last fifty years. The
temptation is to think that Nev and Auerbach are a pair
of photographic positives printed from Vladislavić and his
sometime collaborator Goldblatt. But this book is obsessed
with imperfect doublings and it comes with its own caveat
emptor: 'Stratagems banged around the truth like moths
around an oil lamp.' Things are not what they seem, and
this is not a roman à clef, though it has been expertly
rigged to look like one.

With a language as scintillating and fine-grained as a
silver gelatin print, Vladislavić delivers something rarer
and subtler than a novelization of experience: he gives us,
in this soft, sly novel, 'the seductive mysteries of things as
they are'. At heart, the novel is about an encounter between
two great intellects in an evil time. It is an account of a
sentimental education, though there's a quickness to the
narrative that allows it to elude such categorical confine-
ment. The sceptical, hot-blooded and quick-tongued younger
man and the reticent, unsentimental and deceptively stolid

veteran navigate their way through a brutal time in a brutal place. Neither of them is politically certain – that rawness of response is outsourced in part to a visiting British journalist who goes out on a shoot with them – but both are ethically engaged, and both realize how deeply perverse their present order (South Africa in the 1980s) is. 'It could not be improved upon,' Nev says of that time; 'it had to be overthrown.' This young Nev is self-certain but unsteady on his feet. We are reminded that he is, as his name tells us, a Lister. He pitches forward. 'I felt that I was swaying slightly, the way you do after a long journey when the bubble in an internal spirit level keeps rocking even though your body has come to rest.' Vladislavić's prose is vibrant: it is alert to vibrations, movement and feints, as though it were fitted with a secret accelerometer.

Double Negative is in three parts, dealing respectively with youth, a return from exile and maturity. The plot is light: through the drift of vaguely connected incident, all set down as though remembered, Vladislavić draws the reader into a notion that this is a memoir. But these are stories about an invented self interacting with other invented persons. It is not recollection – but it is also not not recollection. It is a double negative. What sustains this enterprise, and sustains it magnificently, is Vladislavić's narrative intelligence, nowhere more visible than in his way with language itself. Each section is perfectly judged; we enter incidents in medias res – as though they were piano études – and exit them before we have overstayed our welcome.

Above all, there is in *Double Negative*, as in all Vladislavić's writing, an impressive facility with metaphor. Metaphors provide the observational scaffolding on which the story is set. They also occasion much of Vladislavić's finest writing in this finely written book: someone has 'three wooden clothes pegs with their teeth in the fabric of her dress and they moved with her like a shoal of fish'; 'a window display of spectacles looked on like a faceless crowd'; barbershop clients 'reclined with their necks in slotted basins like aristocrats on the scaffold'; somebody 'faded into the background like a song on the radio'; and, impishly signalling his own technique, lenses on a pair of black-rimmed glasses are 'as thick as metaphors'.

In the 1980s, the scholars George Lakoff and Mark Johnson argued that metaphor is pervasive in the English language and that our penchant for metaphorical speech creates the structures of social interaction. But in Vladislavić's hands, the metaphor goes beyond this quotidian utility and, refreshed, reconstructed and revived, does a great deal more: it becomes a ferry for the uncanny, a deployment of images so exact that the ordinary becomes strange and the strange familiar. Metaphors are at home in South Africa's strange and sad history, where many things are like many other things, but nothing is quite the same as anything else.

A metaphor is semantic. A double negative, on the other hand, is syntactical: two negations together in a sentence usually lead to an affirmation (in the wrong places, they could be merely an intensified negation). But a double negative, in the sense of two wrongs making a right, is a form of strategic longwindedness. To use two terms of negation to say that something is 'not unlike' something else is not the same as saying it is like that thing. Double negatives register instances of self-cancelling misdirection. They are about doubt, the productive and counterproductive aspects of doubt, the pitching ground, the listing figure, and the little gap between intention and effect.

Beyond the grammatical sense of 'double negative', Vladislavić wants us to think of the photographic negative, upside down, its colours flipped, its habitation of the dark. Its double, the printed photograph, is the right side up, with a system of colours and shadows that resembles our world, and a form that invites viewing in the light. 'A photograph is an odd little memorial that owes a lot to chance and intuition', Auerbach says. But a photograph is also a little machine of ironies that contains a number of oppositions: light and dark, memory and forgetting, ethics and injustice, permanence and evanescence. There is an echo of 'double negative' in the term given to a photographic negative that has been exposed twice before it is developed: a 'double exposure'. In a double exposure, two instances of light, two photographic events, are registered in a single frame. Nev's return to the places he visited with Auerbach, and his superimposition of two sets of memories on a single location in Johannesburg, are a kind of double exposure, too.

Late in the novel, a grown-up Nev Lister talks to his wife Leora about a recent interview:

> 'She was being ironic, obviously,' she said.
> 'Yes.'
> 'And so are you.'
> 'I guess.'
> 'The whole thing is ironic.'
> 'Including the ironies.'
> 'Maybe they cancel one another out then,' Leora said, 'Like a double negative.'

Teju Cole
New York, May 2013

AVAILABLE LIGHT

Just when I started to learn something, I dropped out of university, although this makes it sound more decisive than it was. I slipped sideways. After two years of English Literature and Classics, not to mention History, Sociology and Political Science, as we used to call it, my head grew heavy and I no longer wanted to be a student. Once my studies were over I would have to go to the army, which I did not have the stomach for either, so I registered for my majors at the beginning of the academic year and stopped going to lectures. When my father found out, he was furious. I was wasting my time and his money. The fact that I was living under his roof again, after a year or two of standing on my own feet, made it worse.

How can I explain it now? I wanted to be in the real world, but I wasn't sure how to set about it. My studies had awakened a social conscience in me, on which I was incapable of acting. So I wandered around in town, seeing imperfection and injustice at every turn, working myself into a childish temper, and then I went home and criticized my parents and their friends. We sat around the dinner table arguing about wishy-washy liberalism and the wages of domestic workers while Paulina, who had been with my family since before I was born, clattered the dishes away through the serving hatch.

After an argument in which my father threatened to cut off my allowance, I drove over to the Norwood Hypermarket, in the Datsun he'd bought me for my eighteenth birthday, to look at the community notice board. Most of the adverts for part-time employment were for students, which suited me. Technically, I was still a student, while having no real studies to pursue made me flexible.

I flipped through the handwritten notices with their gap-toothed fringes of telephone numbers. Door-to-door salesmen, envelope stuffers, waiters. It might be amusing to watch the middle classes fattening themselves for the slaughter. 'Record shop assistant' was appealing: I knew someone who worked Saturday mornings at Hi-Fi Heaven and she always had the latest albums. But it all seemed so bourgeois. I wanted to get my hands dirty. I would have gone picking tomatoes if that had been an option, following the seasonal harvest like some buddy of Jack Kerouac's.

The ad that caught my eye looked like a note from a serial killer. Not everyone was a graphic artist in those days, a cut-and-paste job still took a pair of scissors and a pot of glue. I tore a number from a full row.

•

Jaco Els painted lines and arrows in parking lots. This kind of work was usually done with brushes and rollers; Jaco was faster and cheaper with a spray gun and stencils. He got more work than he could handle on his own.

First impressions? He was my idea of a snooker player, slim and pointed, and a bit of a dandy. Slightly seedy too. He gave me a powdery handshake while he sized me up, working out an angle. Later I discovered that he had acquired the chalky fingertips in the line of duty.

Jaco himself did the skilled part of the job, for what it was worth. He wielded the gun and managed the tanks, which were mounted on the back of a maroon Ranchero. My job was to move the stencils and do the touching up. The stencils were made of hardboard and hinged in the middle for easy transport and storage. They opened and closed like books, oversized versions of the ones I was trying to get away from. This was a library of unambiguous signs. Turn left, turn right, go straight. On a good day, we repeated these simple messages on tar and cement a hundred times.

Being a worker was even harder than I'd hoped. I pinched a dozen blood blisters into my fingers on the first day and breathed in paint fumes until I reeled. The next day I brought along gloves and a mask from my father's workshop. We had to *wikkel*, as Jaco put it. A section of a parking garage would be beaconed off or a lane on a ramp closed while we painted, and it had to be done on the double. Together we marked out the positions with a chalk line, and then Jaco sprayed while I set out the stencils and touched up the edges with a roller. From time to time, he would move the van and turn over the tape. Music to work by.

Within fifteen minutes of meeting him, I learned that he had employed a string of black assistants before me. 'None of them could take the punch,' he said. 'Now I don't mind working on my own, hard graft never killed anyone, but I'm a person who needs company.' You mean an audience, I thought, a witness. 'I reckon it's worth laying out a bit extra and having someone to shoot the breeze with when I'm on the road.' No black labourer would have ridden in the cab, of course, he would have gone on the back like a piece of equipment.

My new boss was a storyteller with a small, vicious gift: he knew just how to spin out a yarn and tie a slip knot in its end. 'You're bloody lucky you've still got to go to the army,' he told me. 'My camps are over. I volunteered for more, but the brass said no. Suppose they've got to give lighties like you a chance to get shot.' He was full of stories about floppies and terrs. Once he got going, you couldn't stop him. Chilled as I was by the brutality of these stories, they drew me in, time and again, and even made me laugh. In the evenings, as I rubbed the paint off my hands with turps in my mother's laundry, among piles of scented sheets and towels, I felt queasily complicit. But I told myself that this was also part of the real world. I was seeking out bitter lessons, undergoing trials of a minor sort, growing up. Such things were necessary.

Strangely enough, of all the violent stories Jaco told me, the one that comes back to me now has nothing to do with the war on the border or patrols in the townships. It concerns a woman who caught the heel of her shoe in the hem of her dress as she alighted from a Putco bus, and fell, and knocked the teeth out of the plastic comb she was holding in her hand.

Jaco and I drove from one end of Johannesburg to the other with *Hotel California* blaring from the speakers. The knives were out but the beast would not die. A revolution was afoot in the retail world: the age of the mall was dawning (although we had not heard the term yet). Corner shops were making way for new shopping centres, and the pioneering ones, already a decade old, were growing. The parking garages were growing too. Jaco could not have been happier. We drove and drove, he talked and I listened, and then I scrambled for the stencils, hurling them open like the Books of the Law, and he zapped them with the spray gun. Turn left, turn right, go straight. It tickled him when I didn't get out of the way in time and he put a stripe of red or yellow over my wrist.

There were hours of calm pleasure, when Jaco went off to buy paint or do his banking, or more secretive duties in the service of the state that he hinted at too broadly, and left me behind in some parking lot to join the dots. Working alone, in silence, I sometimes thought I was achieving something after all. In my jackson-pollocked overalls – I had to stop Paulina from washing the history out of them – in a clearing among the cars defined by four red witch's hats, I was a solitary actor on a stage: a white boy playing a black man. In a small way, I was a spectacle. Yet I felt invisible. I savoured the veil that fell between my sweaty self and the perfumed women sliding in and out of their cars. I flitted across the lenses of their dark glasses like a spy.

One afternoon, I was painting little arcs in the parking area at Hyde Square, turning the sets of parallel lines between the bays into islands, when there was a bomb scare in the centre. Businessmen ran out through the glass doors clutching serviettes like white flags. And then a woman in a plastic cape with half her hair in curlers, who looked as if she had risen from the operating table in the middle of brain surgery with part of her head missing. Everyone flapped about, outraged and delighted, full of righteous alarm. Model citizens. Along the façade of the building was a mural, a line of black figures on a white background, and this separate-but-equal crowd drew my attention. They looked on solemnly, although their eyes were popping. The masses, I thought, the silent majority, observing this self-important European anxiety with Assyrian calm. I took my cue from them. I went on nudging new paint into the cracks in the tar, cold-blooded, maliciously pleased.

The bomb turned out to be a carry case of bowls left behind by an absent-minded pensioner.

In time, Jaco's stories got to me. I could laugh off the knowing asides on brainwashing and espionage, which were straight out of *The Ipcress File*, but the nightlife in Otjiwarongo was less amusing the third time around. It shamed me that I said nothing when he launched into one of his routines. Why was I silent? If I am honest, it had nothing to do with needing the money or enjoying the work: I was scared of him.

When I was living in a student house in Yeoville, we had played a party game, an undergraduate stunt called 'The Beerhunter'. A game of chance for six players. It was Benjy, I think, who picked it up on a trip to the States as an exchange student. The ringmaster would take a single can out of a six-pack of beers and give it a good shake. Then the loaded can was mixed in with the others and each player had to choose one and open it next to his head.

Jaco was like a can that had been shaken. For all his jokey patter, he was full of dangerous energies, and if you prodded him in the wrong place, he would go off pop. He pointed the spray gun like a weapon. He was a small man, but he made a fist as round and hard as a club, spattered with paint and freckles. I could see him using it to *donner* me, the way he *donnered* everyone else in his stories.

While this was happening, my parents acquired new neighbours. Louis van Huyssteen was a young public prosecutor, just transferred to Johannesburg from his home town of Port Elizabeth. He had a wife called Netta and two small children.

The first thing that struck us about them was how much they braaied. 'It's a holiday thing,' my father said. 'When the chap goes back to work in January, it'll stop.' But they picked up the pace instead. 'Perhaps they still have to connect the stove,' my mother said, 'or organize the kitchen?'

That was not it. They simply liked their meat cooked on an open fire. Minutes after Louis came in from work, long enough to kick off his shoes and pull on a pair of shorts, a biblical column of smoke would rise from their yard, and before long the smell of meat roasting on the coals wafted through the hedge that separated their place from ours. The braai was an old-fashioned one fit to feed an army, half of a 44-gallon drum mounted on angle-iron legs, standing close beside the kitchen door. Often, Netta would lean there in the doorway holding a paring knife or sit on the back step with a bowl in her lap, and they would chat while he turned the meat over on the grill. Once I watched him pump the mince out of a dozen sausages, squeezing

them in his fist so that the filling peeled out at either end
and tossing the skins on the coals. And I saw her lift the
folds of her skirt and do a little bump-and-grind routine
to an undertone of music, until he pulled her close and
slid his hands between her thighs. It sounds like I used to
spy on them, I know.

When it came to outdoor living we were not in the
same league, but we had the patio and the pool, and my
dad could char a lamb chop as well as the next man, so
when my mother decided to invite the new neighbours
over to break the ice, a pool-side party was the obvious
arrangement.

Jaco and I worked on Saturdays – we could get a lot
done in the afternoons after the shops closed – and the
braai was nearly over when I got home. Usually I flopped
into the pool to wash off the sweat and dust of the day,
but the Van Huyssteens' sun-browned kids were splashing
in the deep end. The toddler could swim like a fish. Her
brother, who was a few years older, was dive-bombing her
off the end of the filter housing. They looked unsinkable.

I remembered my mother's remark, some personal
history gleaned when she went next door to invite them
over: 'They used to live near the aquarium.'

By the time I had showered, the girl was asleep on the
couch with the damp flex of her hair coiled on a velveteen

cushion. The boy was reading a photo comic, lying on his back on the parquet near the door, where I used to lie myself when I was his age, keeping cool in the hot weather. Brother and sister. They made the house seem comfortably inhabited. I was grateful suddenly for the parquet; my dad was making money in the craze for wall-to-wall carpets, but he couldn't stand them himself, said they turned any room into a padded cell. Stepping through the sliding doors on to the patio, I paused to feel the heat in the slasto on my soles, enjoying the contrast, and thought: perfect. A perfect summer evening. A breeze carried the scent of my mother's roses from the side of the house, moths and beetles made crazy orbits around the moon of the lamp, the pool water shifted in its sleep like a well-fed animal, breathing out chlorine. The sky over the rooftops, where the last of the light was seeping into the horizon, was a rare pink. The seductive mysteries of things as they are, the scent of the roses and the pale stain in the west ran together in my senses.

I can picture myself there, long-haired and bravely bearded, in patched jeans and a T-shirt. The smell of that evening is still in my clothes.

My parents and their guests were talking, and you could tell by the sated murmur of conversation, the outstretched legs and tilted heads, that the meal had been good. My mother had put something aside for me, although there was so much left over it hardly seemed necessary. While

I was helping myself to salads, I heard Netta ask for the chicken marinade recipe and my mother fetched an airmail letter pad and wrote it out for her. The recipe was a sort of family secret – it had been devised by Charlie, my Auntie Ellen's houseboy – but it was shared often and eagerly. Usually, Charlie's idiosyncrasies were part of the rigmarole of handing on the secret, but tonight my mother made no mention of him at all.

My father and Louis were hanging around the braai, as the men must, and I joined them there with my heaped plate. My dad had a little cocktail fridge from the caravan set up on the patio and I fetched a Kronenbräu from the icy cave of its freezer. The dessert was already on the coals: bananas wrapped in foil. Louis had commandeered the tongs. As he turned the packages idly, the smell of cinnamon and brown sugar melted into the overburdened air.

For a long time the talk was about children, the neighbourhood, the new house, the quality of the local primary school, things I did not have much to say about. I busied myself with the food, drank the beer too quickly, fetched another one. My father told Louis about the new wall-to-wall carpet lines and the problems in the factory with the union. 'But enough shop talk,' he said, and moved on to the caravan park in Uvongo where they'd spent their last holiday. It was the height of luxury: there was a power point at every site so you could plug in your generator. 'The newer vans are moving to electricity. One of these

days gas will be a thing of the past, you mark my words.'
Then they argued playfully about the relative merits of the
South Coast and the Cape as holiday destinations. My father
ribbed him a little, and demonstrated that he could speak
Afrikaans – *'Julle Kapenaars,'* he kept saying – and Louis took
it all in good humour.

It might have gone on like this, until my mom put the
leftover wors in a Tupperware and the Van Huyssteens said
thank you very much, what a lovely day, and went home.
But of course it didn't.

At some point, Louis slipped into the repetitive storytelling I had to endure every day as I drove around Joburg
with Jaco Els. The shift was imperceptible, as if someone
had put on a record in the background, turned down low,
and by the time you became aware of it your mood had
already altered. An odourless poison leaked out of him. His
dearest childhood memories were of the practical jokes he
had played on the servants. Stringing ropes to trip them
up, setting off firecrackers under their beds, unscrewing
the seat on the long drop. You could imagine that he had
found his vocation in the process. His work, which involved
jailing people for petty offences, was a malevolent prank.
The way he spoke about it, forced removals, detention
without trial, the troops in the townships were simply
larger examples of the same mischief.

I was struck by the intimacy of his racial obsession.
His prejudice was a passion. It caused him an exquisite

sort of pain, like worrying a loose tooth with your tongue or scratching a mosquito bite until it bleeds.

In the mirror of his stories, however, the perspective was reversed. While he was always hurting someone, doing harm and causing trouble, he saw himself as the victim. All these people he didn't like, these inferior creatures among whom he was forced to live, made him miserable. It was he who suffered. I understand this better now than I did then. At the time, I was trying to grasp my own part in the machinery of power and more often than not I misjudged the mechanism. *Seid Sand, nicht das Öl im Getriebe der Welt*, my friend Sabine had told me. *Seid unbequem.* Be troublesome. Be sand, not oil in the workings of the world. Sand? Must I be ground down to nothing? Should I let myself be milled? It was abject. Surely one could be a spanner in the works rather than a handful of dust? I'd rather be a hammer than a nail.

These thoughts were driven from my mind by Louis's suffering face, the downturned lips, the wincing eyes. Even his crispy hair looked hurt. You could see it squirming as he combed it in the mornings, gazing mournfully at his face in the shaving mirror.

I could have shouted at him. 'Look around you! See how privileged we are. We've all eaten ourselves sick, just look at the debris, paper plates full of bones and peels, crumpled serviettes and balls of foil, bloody juices. And yet we haven't made a dent in the supply.' The dish on the edge of the fire was full of meat, thick chops and coils of wors soldered to the stainless steel with grease. The fat of the land was still sizzling on the blackened bars of the grill. You would think the feast was about to begin.

I knew what had produced this excess. Through the leaves of the hedge, light gleamed on the bonnet of Louis's new Corolla, sitting in his driveway like an enormous piece of evidence.

I should have challenged him to play the Beerhunter. We were drunk enough by then and he had the face for it. Instead, I decided to argue with him, as if we had just come out of a seminar with Professor Sherman and were debating some point in Marx on the library lawns. The details escape me now, they're not important. Racialized capital, the means of production, the operation of the military-industrial complex, I was full of it. 'Just imagine,' I remember saying, 'that you've worked all your life down a bloody gold mine and you still can't afford to put food on the table for your family. Can you imagine? No you can't. That's the problem.'

'The commies at Wits have spoken a hole in your head,' was the gist of his reply. 'What do you know about the world? When you've lived a bit, seen a few things, you'll know better. If your black brothers ever get hold of this country, they'll run it into the ground. It's happened everywhere in Africa.'

My father cracked a few jokes and tried to change the subject. When that failed, he gave me a pointed look, a stare that seemed to stretch out his features and make his nose long and sharp. It was the look he used to give me as a boy when I wouldn't listen. Go to your room, it said. *Now.* Before I lose my temper.

We went from calling each other names to pushing and shoving like schoolboys behind the bicycle sheds. Out of the corner of my eye, I saw Netta getting to her feet and my mother turning in her chair to see what the commotion was about.

Louis had what Jaco liked to call a *donner my gesig.* His sorry mug was begging to be hit. I would have done it, I suppose. Apparently I raised the beer bottle like a club. But before I could go further, my father slapped me hard through the face. One blow was all it took to knock the world back into order. Louis straightened his shirt and his mouth. I was told to apologize, which I did. We shook hands.

Then, in fact, I went to my room.

On the way, I stopped in the bathroom to splash my face with cold water. There was a red mark on my jaw. My father was all talk when it came to discipline. He would unbuckle his belt and say, 'Do you want me to give you a hiding?' Don't be ridiculous. He had never raised a hand to me. That he had hit me at all was as shocking as the blow itself. I found the shapes of his fingers on my cheek like the map of a new country.

The Van Huyssteens stayed for coffee, to avoid the implication that the whole day had been a catastrophe.

Later, I heard them gathering up the sleeping children, *Ag shame* and *Oh sweet*, and going down the driveway. It was the last time they ever set foot in my parents' house.

Voices rumbled in the kitchen. Then my father came into my room.

I was still a little drunk or perhaps I was drunk again. The room was drifting, and so I stayed where I was on my bed, with my hands behind my neck, insolent. I was ready to be furious, but the look on his face made it impossible.

'I'm sorry, my boy,' he said.

'It's okay.'

'You understand that I had to do this? I couldn't have you hitting a visitor in this house.'

'Ja.'

'You were spoiling for a fight.'

Spoiling. To spoil for a fight. What exactly does it mean?

'I had to hit someone.'

'Then you should have hit *him*,' I said. 'He was asking for it. Fucking fascist.'

I imagine the expletive was more surprising to my father than the political persuasion, which I had been bandying about lately.

'Perhaps. But you don't settle your differences with your fists. Not under this roof.'

We spoke a bit longer. My father made a joke about watching your step around Afrikaners with law degrees. Never *klap* a BJuris! Finally, he reached out to show me something in his palm. It was a moment before I understood the gesture. When I stood up to take his hand, I saw that there were tears in his eyes.

My father's remorse lasted for a week. Then one evening he called me into his study, sat me down in the chair facing his desk as if I were a sales rep who'd pranged the company car, and read me the Riot Act.

My argument with Louis had given him the jitters. The family motto had always been: 'Don't rock the boat.' He was worried, although he did not express it in so many words, that I would get involved in politics, that I would fall in with the wrong crowd. There was really little danger of that. Politics confounded me. The student politicians I had encountered were full of alarming certitudes. By comparison, my own position was always wavering. I was too easily drawn to the other person's side. Half the time I was trying to convince myself, through my posturing, that I knew what I was talking about, that I got it.

I went to demonstrations against detention without trial, the pass laws, forced removals. I helped to scrawl slogans on sheets of cardboard and carry them over to Jan Smuts Avenue. But then I hung back, making sure there were two or three students to hide behind. My girlfriend Linda was always in front; her parents were proud of her for doing these things. I was not made for the front line.

The police on the opposite kerb scared me, it's true, but I was more afraid of the men with cameras and flashguns. I did not want to see my photograph in the security police files. More importantly, I did not want to see it, I did not want anyone else to see it, on the front page of the *Rand Daily Mail*.

The world beyond the campus, where the real politicians operated rather than the student replicas, was a mystery to me. Realpolitik. The new term with its foreign accent clarified nothing. People I knew from campus, writers on the student paper, the members of theatre companies and vegetable co-ops, were finding their way into the Movement, as they called it, but I had no idea how to seek out such a path, and no inclination either, to be honest. The Movement. It sounded like a machine, not quite a juggernaut but a piece of earthmoving equipment for running down anyone who stood in the way, crushing the obstacles pragmatically into the churned-up demolition site of history. Construction site, they would have insisted.

Towards the end of my university days, a farmer near the Botswana border drove his bakkie over a landmine and his daughter was killed. The newspapers carried photographs of the child's body and the parents' anguish. The gory details. Soon afterwards, an activist recently released from prison came to speak on campus. He spoke passionately, provocatively, about the bitter realities of the struggle, quoting Lenin on revolutionary violence without mentioning his name. 'There will be casualties,' he said more than once. When a girl in the audience questioned the killing of soft targets, the murder of babies, he rounded on her as if she were a spoilt child: 'This isn't a party game – it's a revolution! There are no innocent bystanders.' She sat down as if she'd been slapped.

Thoughts like these must have run through my mind while my father was lecturing me about dirty politics and the things the security police did to detainees at John Vorster Square. He was looking for reassurance, you see, but I felt it necessary to fuel his unease, acting up, dropping in phrases from books – 'the ruling class' – repeating points made by radical students on the hustings during SRC elections. The need to Africanize ourselves and our culture, the morality of taking up arms against an oppressive regime, colonialism of a special kind. I may have mentioned Frelimo. No doubt I quoted Prof Sherman – Hegemony Cricket, we used to call him.

The button eyes in the leather couch winked as if they were in on the game.

After a while my father changed the subject. He began to talk about my national service. 'If you're not planning to go back to university,' he said, 'you should go into the army in July. Get it over with sooner.' He knew my feelings on this subject. He was just reminding me of the unpleasant consequences of my decisions and it was a pretty good strategy. I began to watch my words.

The talk wound down. When I was on the point of leaving, he said, 'Are you busy Thursday?'

'Well, I'm working with Jaco as usual.'

'Take a day's leave. Tell him you have to go to a funeral. There's something I want you to do for me.'

It was not a question. My first thought was that he wanted me to help with the stocktaking in the warehouse, which I'd done before, but he had something else in mind. He pushed a large book across the desk.

'Have you heard of Saul Auerbach?'

The photograph on the cover looked familiar.

'He's a photographer, a very good one. Also happens to be a friend of your Uncle Douglas.'

Now I placed the photo. There was a copy of it in my uncle's lounge. It had caught my eye mainly because I was not used to seeing a photograph framed and hung on the wall like a painting.

'Doug's arranged for you to spend Thursday with Saul. He's doing some work around the city and he's kindly agreed to let you ride along.'

'What for?'

'I think it will be good for you. You might even learn something.'

'I don't want to be a photographer.'

'That doesn't matter. It's not about finding a profession, you'll make your own way in the end, I'm sure. It's about this anger you're walking around with, this bottled-up rage against the world. It worries me: it's going to land you in trouble. And that's why you might learn something from Saul. He's a man with strong convictions, but he's learned to direct them.'

'I don't even know the guy.'

My father tapped on the book. 'Just look at the pictures.'

If you want to find out about Saul Auerbach, go ahead and google him. He has three pages on Wikipedia and gets a mention on dozens of photography sites. Saulauerbach.com, which is maintained by his agent, has the basic facts of his career. If you're after the details, there are blogs devoted to particular periods of his work and squabbles about its merits. Specialized search engines will guide you to his photographs in museums and you can find others scattered in online journals and galleries. Writing a paper? There are articles, freely accessible or available for purchase, on his style, his influences, his politics, on his use of black and white, on the question of whether he is a photographer or an artist or both. Planning to buy? Getart.com offers investment advice. If, after all this, you still need a book on the subject, the online retailers will show you what's in print and bookHound will direct you to the bargains. You could become an expert on Auerbach without getting up from your desk.

In those days, before everyone's life was an open secret, research involved a trip to a library or a newspaper archive, and the pickings were often slim. While I was curious about Auerbach, I did not have time to find out who he was. They might have had something about him in the Wartenweiler on campus, but I did not want to go there. I had declared the university out of bounds.

All I had was the pictures. I sat on my bed, with the book propped against my knees, and flipped through it. It was a great book, according to my father (quoting my uncle, the artistic side of the family). I had no way of telling, although I was ready to disagree. Between the covers were two hundred of Auerbach's photographs: he had made the selection himself. The images were dense and sunken, they seemed to have settled beneath the glossy surfaces like gravestones. These black and white boxes weighed on me. Worlds had been compacted into them and sealed in oil. If I tilted the book the wrong way and exposed some pinhole to the air, they might burst into their proper dimensions. I imagined one of these rooms inhaling, filling itself with life, breaking back into scale with a crack of stage lightning. The images were familiar and strange. I kept looking at a hand or a foot, a shoe, the edge of a sheet turned back, the street name painted on a kerb. Have I been here? Is this someone I'm going to meet? I turned the pages with the unsettling feeling that I had looked through the book before and forgotten.

The title page was inscribed: 'To Doug and Ellen, with my very best wishes and thanks for your kindness and support, Saul, 12th September 1980.' The book had been closed before the ink dried and fragments of the letters had come off on the opposite page, lightly curved strokes like eyelashes. What kind of support had my uncle given Saul Auerbach? Auntie Ellen was a music teacher and dancer of note, prone to demonstrating her skills extravagantly at family weddings when she'd had one too many. Perhaps she'd taught Auerbach to rumba in an unguarded moment.

In the flap of the dust jacket I found a handful of exhibition reviews clipped from newspapers and magazines, none more than a few paragraphs long. One reviewer spoke about the rigour of Auerbach's composition and his fine understanding of light. Another praised his dispassionate eye but questioned the grimness of the images it gave rise to. A third, more enthusiastic offering from *Scenario* said that the humanity of Auerbach's vision transcended politics and enabled a deep engagement with his subjects.

I read the reviews twice, trying to see if or how they contradicted one another. Was technical proficiency an element of style, perspective or personality? Could one be dispassionate and deeply engaged at the same time? I paced through the book, going to the edge of the world and back, over and over, without finding an answer.

'Why does the old man want me to meet this Auerbach guy? What's he up to?'

My father had gone to his Sunday morning golf game, my mother was baking – cheese straws, one of her specialities – rolling out the dough on a board at the kitchen table. She looked at me over her glasses while she floured the rolling pin. 'He thinks it will be interesting for you, Nev. Instructive. He's at the top of his field, you know.'

'What must I do?'

'Just tag along, watch, learn, I don't know.'

'I already told Dad I'm not planning to become a photographer.' I had belonged briefly to the camera club at high school and learned to do my own developing, but it was never more than a hobby, and given up faster than philately. It was years since I'd taken more than a holiday snap.

'More's the pity,' my mother said. 'You've got a good eye. Even Mr Marshall said so and he wasn't free with his compliments.'

My high-school art master, old Marshall Arts himself. In fact, he'd done nothing to discourage me when I dropped his subject in Standard 8 to do Latin. My father was still hoping then that I would study Law.

'Do you know Auerbach?'

'I've met him once or twice, in passing. He was at the theatre once with Ellen and she introduced us.'

'What's he like?'

'You should really talk to Dad about this, it was his idea.' She dipped a knife in the flour packet and made four long cuts through the dough, carving out a perfect square and sweeping the ragged edges aside. When she was done, she would knead the offcuts together into another ball, dust the board and the pin, and roll it out again. Waste not, want not. 'I'm sure it's not about the photographs at all but Saul's way of doing things. He's famously patient, quite happy to wait all day until the light strikes a wall just so, a total professional. Maybe he can teach you something about perseverance, learning to do one thing properly. Your father is very disappointed that you've dropped out. And this whole line-painting business, he thinks it's beneath you, and I agree. We've given you a bit of time to find yourself – but you're getting lost instead.'

When he spoke about things like this, my father always used the word 'gumption'. A word that stuck to the roof of your mouth like peanut butter.

I gathered that Auerbach was supposed to teach me a lesson about life. He was to be an example to me (we did not say 'role model' then).

There had to be more to it than that. Between them, my father and my uncle must have briefed the man about me. Me and my problems. He would give me a talking-to, this gloomy stranger. I was irritated with him before we even met.

Moving back to Bramley was not a good idea. The year before, my girlfriend Linda and I had shared a room in a house in Yeo Street, but when she decided to finish her studies in Cape Town, we parted company. The relationship had run its course. Our housemates were graduating and starting jobs or going abroad, and so the house broke up too. I might have found a place in another commune, but the thought of dropping out was already in my mind and I moved back under my parents' roof instead. It was convenient and cheap, but I would have done better taking a flat on my own.

How could I not feel like a child here? To be reminded of how young I really was, I had only to glance at the jamb of my bedroom door, where a succession of dates and heights scored on the paint in different inks, rising year by year, charted my physical growth to the age of sixteen. Just a few years ago. That ladder, observed from my bed with an open book forgotten on my chest, would draw my eye up into the heights of the room, where two model aeroplanes were suspended in perpetual combat against the blank sky of the ceiling. A Messerschmitt and a Spitfire. There had been others, Flying Fortresses, Stukas, Bristol Blenheims, but they had all gone down in flames over the years, leaving a solitary dogfight. I had built the planes myself from kits and suspended them on fishing line. They never turned out like the pictures on the boxes: you got glue all over the cockpit glass, and the decals, the impudent English bullseyes and angular German crosses, went on skew or came apart on your fingertips. But from a distance they were convincing enough. It was part of the training of ground-to-air gunners, my grandpa told me, to learn the distinctive silhouettes of aircraft, your own as well as the enemy's.

I had tidied away my childhood, but traces remained. The Hardy Boys had migrated to the bottom of the bookshelf to make space for my university textbooks. A NUSAS poster about forced removals was taped to the wardrobe door, alongside Joanna Lumley in a leotard and tights, packing a pistol. Linda laughed out loud the first time she saw it and then I refused to part with it on principle. The imitation-leather beanbag I'd picked up along the way was squashed into a corner. My spray painter's mask and gloves lay on the pine desk where I'd crammed for my matric exams. At my mother's insistence, I stored the overalls in the garage. Even so, there was a fume of turpentine in the air.

In these clashing currents, on the eve of my meeting with Auerbach, I leafed morosely through his book. What was he hiding? What had he missed?

I parked the Datsun in the street outside Auerbach's house in Craighall Park and waited for five to nine. I would give him no excuse to find fault. The house was low-lying and roughly plastered, set in a garden full of old trees. There was something Mediterranean about the dappled pergolas, the walls as creamy as feta, the succulent shadows of fig leaves and thick-tongued aloes cast by the late-summer sun. Years later, I read in Chipkin's book that it was House Something-or-Other, named for the original owner, and that the architect was quite famous for his Hellas on the Highveld mannerisms.

Auerbach answered the doorbell and showed me through to the kitchen. He was matter-of-fact to the point of rudeness, as I expected. 'No nonsense' was the phrase my father had used.

A still life on the kitchen counter: apples in a wooden bowl shaped like a dhow, two quarters of lemon on a ceramic tile decorated with a spiral, salt in a finger bowl. Ritual objects, I thought.

'Breakfast?'

'I've eaten thanks.'

A slice of toast sprang up on the counter. While he was buttering it, I had time to glance into the lounge, a cool cavern of honeyed slate floors and paper-white walls that set off dark linocuts and African masks in smoky wood, rough-hewn creatures with horns, apparently bootblacked, a beaded doll. Kilims, leather, a bit of chrome. A dated modern style that suited him.

'Coffee then?'

'Yes please.'

I had never seen a cafetière before. He leaned on the plunger and gazed out of the window. It seemed to me that he was doing it in slow motion, building up tension in the room along with the mass of grounds in the bottom of the pot, drawing attention to the device. But why? After a minute in his company I felt off balance, provoked to speculate about trifles.

I sat at the table with my coffee while he picked through his camera bags to make sure everything was there, fetched odd pieces of equipment from other rooms, pausing every now and then to take a bite out of the toast or eat a segment of orange. He was a family man, as I knew from the dust jacket of his book, but there was no sign of a wife or child. You would have thought he lived on his own. He was excessively crumpled, in khaki shorts and a shirt with epaulettes and brass buttons left over from the North Africa campaign. An old soldier. My father's age, I guessed, but my dad would have looked plump and office-bound beside him.

The car in the driveway was a Rambler, more than a few years old. He packed the gear into the boot – refusing my offer of help on the grounds that it would disrupt his rhythm – and we drove into the city.

'You're at Wits?'

'I was.'

'Yes, your father tells me you're having second thoughts.'

'I've already dropped out, actually.'

'Why?'

'I'm bored.' This was not strictly true and it sounded spoilt. 'Not bored so much as impatient. I want to get on with my life. Do things.'

'Life will get on with you soon enough,' he said, 'you shouldn't be in such a cast-iron hurry.'

Then I expected him to ask: 'So what are you going to do?' But he did not.

He drove with careless expertise, as if his mind were on other things, weaving through the traffic along Jan Smuts Avenue, gunning the car into empty space. There was an armrest between us, a soft block of sponge hinged out of the seat-back, and he drummed on it with his left hand as he drove. Stubby fingers, no sign of the taper that Mr Marshall claimed was a sure sign of the artistic temperament. That and nerves. Perhaps the story really was an excuse to hold the boys' hands, as my more suspicious schoolmates used to say. I examined my own hands on my knees. Red crescents under the fingernails, road-marking paint rather than artists' oils.

The silence was stifling. I said bluntly: 'This was my father's idea.'

'I hope he didn't force you to come.'

'Of course not.'

'I could drop you off if you've got something better to do. Just say the word.'

'No, no, it's fine.'

Another pause. 'You know my father.' It was obvious I was making conversation.

'A little. I know Douglas better. We were at varsity together.' He was fiddling with the radio, and before I could answer a pop song burst out of the dash ('like an airbag', I almost said, but that belongs in another period).

The concrete slabs of the Civic Centre stood among flower-trimmed lawns like cinder blocks on an embroidered tea cloth. Some joker had once pointed the place out to me as the municipal mortuary and it was years before I discovered that the trade was in licences and title deeds rather than corpses. I thought of telling Auerbach this story as we dropped down into the city, but evidently he did not appreciate small talk.

He was silent until we pulled up outside the King George in Joubert Park. 'We've got company for the day, journalist by the name of Gerald Brookes, a Brit but a decent fellow. Afraid you'll have to move to the back.'

He crossed the pavement and vanished into the lobby of the hotel.

Listen to me, don't listen to me! Talk to me, don't talk to me! Jesus. He'd left the radio on for my benefit. I turned off the ignition and got out of the car. One of my more imposing affectations was a pipe, a Dr Watson with a bowl the size of an espresso cup; the dropped bowl hung a perpetual question mark on my lip, made me appealingly wry, in my own estimation. I tamped down the crust of my early-morning smoke and sucked the flame of my lighter through it. Then I leaned on the bonnet as the bowl warmed in my palm. Company. I didn't know whether to feel relieved or disappointed.

On the opposite pavement, against the railings of the park, a couple of portrait artists were already waiting hopefully for customers. In midsummer, when the Art Gallery attracted more visitors, there would be half a dozen of them. They set up their easels and camping chairs under the trees every day. I sometimes went past there on my way into town and stopped to watch them working: it was more engaging than the amateur chess on the big outdoor board in the park itself. Chalky old men in berets with dandruff on their collars, and one wild-haired woman with an expressionist mask of a face. She was the only caricaturist among them, a lover of crayon; the others went for realism in pencil, pastel or charcoal. Most had samples of their work sticky-taped to a portfolio leaning against the fence as an advertisement. Usually they showed a photograph and a drawing so that you could judge whether the likeness was true. It was easier to capture someone from a photograph. A photograph was the presentiment of a portrait, stilling an expression, freezing the blood. When the living subject sat before you, breathing, sweating, with an expectant smile budding in the corners of her mouth, it was another matter altogether. Or so I imagined. Perhaps it was the other way round? Perhaps that was precisely what separated the artists from the copyists. The real artists worked from life.

But what did I know?

Auerbach came out of the hotel and went along the pavement with his head down and his fists bunched in the pockets of his shorts. For a moment I thought he was heading off into the city, having forgotten about me entirely. But on the next corner he stopped and looked through a plate-glass window. It was a men's hairdresser, not a barbershop, mind you, but a salon. Marco's or something like that. I had no use for it myself, but I had seen men sitting in there enveloped in linen, getting themselves shaved or coiffed, red linen, as if they expected the worst. Sometimes, the clients reclined with their necks in slotted basins like aristocrats on the scaffold. They actually washed your hair before they cut it. Auerbach stood at the window with his hands peaked over his eyes. He came back. In passing, he tilted his head in my direction, gave an open-handed shrug – And now? – and went back into the hotel.

What do I know?

This question ran like a hairline crack through my thoughts. I had read sociology and political philosophy, I had worked through a few of the key texts of the radical tradition, some of them written in the previous century. In order to read these books, I had sat in a booth in the Cullen Library, where the banned books were kept, as if I were suffering from a contagious disease. My head was like the stacks in the basement of the Cullen. New ideas fell out of old volumes and I tried to unriddle them in the gloom. The air was full of dust. I could scarcely breathe in the space between my ears.

I was in a room with two windows, speaking to myself in Latin – or was it Greek? – about reification and alienation, surplus value and exchange value, base and superstructure. Class consciousness, false consciousness, petit bourgeois, proletarian – the terms fell through a gap between two kinds of knowledge. Through one window I could see the Bolsheviks storming the Winter Palace and Lenin addressing the crowds in Sverdlov Square; through the other, schoolchildren battling the police in the streets of Soweto and Oliver Tambo addressing the General Assembly. Through one, Trotsky and Breton working on their manifesto in Mexico City; through the other, Breytenbach writing poems in his cell at Pretoria Central with a greasepaint moustache on his lip. Tatlin's Monument to the Third International and the Top Star Drive-in. I wanted to bring these views together like the two images in a stereoscope, but I couldn't see through both windows at the same time. I went up and down like a prisoner, until I was dizzy. Finally, I stood in the middle of the room, under the chandelier, with my head aching.

It wasn't a dream: I had never been more awake in my life.

What exactly is the radical tradition? In one of the elections for SRC, a student politician, a long-haired boy from a suburban home like mine, had styled himself as Kropotkin. He went around in a cossack coat and riding boots like an extra from Doctor Zhivago on Ice. And I had nearly voted for him. What to make of Marx with his Boer War beard and his watch chain? He was treated like a patriarch in *War and Peace*, but he was more at home in *David Copperfield*. He might have been a chum of Mr Micawber, always expecting something to turn up.

I am more flippant about this now than I was then. Had you seen me there, with the cold shell of the car against my bum and the morning sun on my face, you would have thought I was an overly earnest young man. You could not see Benjamin's Angel – Klee's Angel, strictly speaking, memorably captioned – leaning beside me with his wings folded across the bonnet. I was troubled. For all my uncertainty about the sacred texts, they had dumped me into history and I had a suspicion that I would never be out of it again. Looking back over the brief span of my life, I felt like some object left on the shoreline, toyed with by a rising tide. If you had a sense of historical destiny, if you were sufficiently drunk with it, you might expect to ride out any storm. But I did not imagine I would be carried in one piece to a classless shore. History would break over me like a wave that had already swept through the manor house and bear me off in a jumble of picture frames and paper plates.

•

Gerald Brookes was a red stump of a man with a bald head curiously creased in the middle like an apricot. The lenses of his black-rimmed glasses were as thick as metaphors. He was wearing a black leather jacket belted at the waist and had a camera on a strap around his neck. He was my idea of an East German spy or an ageing bass guitarist. Gerry and the Pacemakers.

As we pulled off, he leaned over the seat and shook my hand. 'Gerry. Saul says you're a journalist in training.'

Auerbach's eye flashed in the rear-view mirror.

'Well, I'm training for something, but I'm not sure what.'

Then they forgot about me. Brookes wanted to know what Auerbach had been up to and he told him. They chatted about mutual friends, new jobs, divorces, property prices. They passed on good wishes and sent regards. Old mates, apparently.

Soon enough they moved on to politics. Brookes was full of questions. Was Botha pushing ahead with the Tricameral Parliament? Would the right-wingers split from the Party? And the extra-parliamentary campaign against the so-called reforms? Was it gathering momentum? What was happening on the ground? Auerbach said he was not really the person to ask, as Brookes should know by now, he could only say what he read in the papers, Brookes was probably better informed than he was. But Brookes insisted: you get around, you speak to people, you've got your finger on the pulse. You must hear things. What are people saying?

'I really don't know.'

'Show me something, baby, I want action,' Brookes said with a peculiar inflection.

'You're a journalist,' Auerbach said. And then, after a pause, 'The action is everywhere.' And he looked out of the window as if something very interesting was happening just then.

We were in Twist Street, waiting for a robot to change. Everything was still. The little red soldier, standing to attention against the black gong of the light, had stopped the world in its tracks. The people on the pavements had their heads turned in different directions, each listening for a signal only they could hear. Across the intersection, a window display of spectacles looked on like a faceless crowd. A skinny man in a floral shirt and an alpine hat made of white raffia was sitting on a bus-stop bench with his hands clasped behind his neck. The second I gazed at him, at the pitted skin of his cheeks, he lurched forward, pulled something from his sock and threw it into a rubbish bin. The lights changed and we took off. Looking back, I saw the man walking swiftly in the other direction.

I wish I could remember clearly what was said that day. Between them, the photographs Auerbach took in the next few hours and my own disordered memories, which by comparison are mere snapshots with the heads cut off and the hands out of focus, have displaced everything else. They hang down like screens I cannot reach behind. I've read a dozen interviews with Auerbach since then, I can imagine what he might have said, but I've done enough ventriloquism as it is.

Duty. That comes back now. They kept circling around it. Thou shalt and thou shalt not. Brookes was obsessed – so it seems in retrospect – with the responsibilities of good people in bad situations, people like Auerbach in places like South Africa, people who were opposed to apartheid. The pros and cons of the cultural boycott, the rights of the individual versus the collective good, the value of contemplation in a state of crisis. How could you go on writing poetry, was the gist of his argument, when you had the wherewithal to take down an affidavit?

Any minute now, I thought, he'll be quoting Adorno, misquoting Adorno, like everyone else. Sabine had written an intricate essay on the subject.

The notion of duty was very much on my mind, not least because I was about to be conscripted. What should I do? Brookes was asking some of the questions I had been trying to formulate for myself ever since it had dawned on me that I was living in a grossly unjust society. But the judgement in his tone riled me. He had all the answers too. He knew exactly how *he* would behave if the two of them traded places. Auerbach did not live up to his standards; he admired him, but he was disappointed in him. He should be doing more for the Movement. He had a duty. I thought of machinery again, an industrial loom for weaving everyone into a single fabric.

Auerbach was adept at answering questions. He must have heard them all before. He insisted on his independence and regretted his limitations as a photographer and a human being. This peculiar passivity also annoyed me. I wanted him to make a better defence of himself and therefore of me. If he was failing in his duty, he should at least be able to explain why. I couldn't speak up for myself. Brookes made it sound so easy to do the right thing, to make a stand, but it was difficult. Wasn't it?

Of course, it didn't come out in one piece like this, I had to put it together afterwards. Through all of this, we were driving. We went to the end of Twist Street, so that Brookes could see the base of the Hillbrow Tower, driven like a stake through a city block. Then we headed for Yeoville. As we went, Auerbach pointed things out and Brookes leaned out of the window and took pictures – of WHITES ONLY benches, separate entrances, a uniformed servant eating her lunch on the kerb. Auerbach's subjects, you could say. In Berea, he got Auerbach to reverse so that he could peer down a service lane where a man and a woman were arguing among the rubbish bins.

Brookes was overheated, he was pink and damp, and I almost felt sorry for him. But he must be a bit thick too, thick-skinned at least, firing away with his Instamatic in the company of a real photographer.

Then, or perhaps it was later in the day, Brookes asked, 'How do you know that a subject is worth photographing?'

Auerbach answered, 'I'm like you: I wait for something to catch my eye.'

'Everything catches my eye,' Brookes laughed. 'You choose your subjects very carefully.'

'Film is expensive.'

Brookes pulled a face.

Then or later, Auerbach said warily, 'The subject draws me, I don't have words for it really, something strikes a chord, rings a bell. Sometimes it's as if I've found a thing I've already seen and remembered, or imagined before, which may not be that different. Perhaps I recognize something in the world as a "picture" when it captures what I've already thought or felt.'

'Evidence.'

'You make it sound like a crime, but it's not that. And it's not proof either, I'm not trying to demonstrate a proposition or substantiate a claim. I'm just looking for what chimes. Let's say there's a disequilibrium in me, my scales are out of kilter, and something out there, along these streets, can right the balance. The photograph – or is it the photographing? – restores order.'

'So it's therapeutic?'

'No, I wouldn't go that far.'

We were parked somewhere. Brookes was half-turned in his seat, looking at Auerbach with an ironic smile, and Auerbach was looking at me in the rear-view mirror. Although he'd been speaking slowly, searching for the right words, his expression was frank.

'Look, if I could explain it to you, then you could take my photographs for me. But you evidently can't. Even if I show you what I do in the darkroom, the tricks of my particular trade, where I like to crop things, the lines that hit the spot, I can't tell you how I see. I can only show you the result. Essentially, the process is beyond explanation and what I say doesn't matter. That's the beauty of it. By the same token – and this is more important – the work is perfectly clear. It's self-explanatory. You should write this down, Ger. It explains itself.'

The presence of a great photographer (to quote my Uncle Douglas), the pressure of his calculating eye, created subject matter. Wherever you looked, you saw a photograph. Not just any photograph either: an Auerbach.

We went down Rockey Street. On Scotch Corner, Auerbach double-parked while Brookes took a photograph of a man in a kilt and platform shoes touting for custom through a megaphone. This black highlander was peering through sunglasses with lenses the size of saucers. Then Brookes wanted to see the water tower on the ridge. He said it was

tripod in *War of the Worlds*, only the heat-ray was
.ng. The whole place was science fiction. 'That's what
people fail to understand about South Africa,' he said. 'It's
a time machine. It's the past's idea of the future.'

'Or vice versa,' Auerbach said.

We took Stewart's Drive down into Bez Valley. Auerbach territory, as I knew from the book. Brookes wanted
to stretch his legs, and so we stopped on a corner with
an Apollo café, a Farmácia and a BP garage, and the two
of them got out. I stayed in the car, brooding over the
discussion earlier, sulking, I suppose. All around, the
houses turned their good sides to the street and held
their breath.

When they came back, Brookes was carrying a paper
bag. While Auerbach aimed the car deeper into the valley,
he rummaged in the bag and took out a can of deodorant.
'If it's good enough for Henry Cooper,' he said, putting on
an accent I couldn't place. He unbuttoned his shirt and
sprayed under his arms.

Auerbach drove us into Kensington. I hardly knew the
area, although I recognized the playing fields at Jeppe Boys,
where I had once kept wicket for a school side. We wound
through smaller streets to Langermann Kop. A track led
to the top of the hill. Auerbach put the shift in low and
we ground up the slope with the *middelmannetjie* scraping
against the bottom of the car. He stopped in a rubble-strewn
clearing and we all piled out.

There was a path going up the koppie that only Auerbach could see, enfolded in veld grass and flowering cosmos.
He plunged in and we followed. Brookes burrowed through
the veld like a glossy black beetle with his jacket creaking
and the camera bumping against his chest. The plume from
a long haulm came off in his teeth and he spat comically.
When we emerged into the open, Auerbach was atop a
rain-streaked outcrop with his hands on his hips, grinning.
The gloomy inwardness of the morning had lifted entirely.
'You won't find a better view of the city,' he called out as
we approached. 'You can see clear to Heidelberg. That's
Jan Smuts over there.'

Beneath us, along the spine of the Reef, the land lay
open like a book. Auerbach pointed out townships and
suburbs, hostels and factories, mine dumps and slimes
dams. His pleasure in the exercise was infectious. Brookes
took some noisy photographs and hopped about, laughing and steaming. He was redder than before. He looked
as if he had just got out of a scalding shower and stepped
straight into his clothes.

We followed our guide back through the grass. Brookes
fetched the paper bag and opened a Fanta orange for each
of us, and we sat on the rocks looking out over Bez Valley
like a gang of schoolboys playing truant. William and Henry
and Ginger. A drowsy calm descended. It was a relief after
the movement and chatter of the past few hours. I felt that
I was swaying slightly, the way you do after a long journey

when the bubble in an internal spirit level keeps rocking even though your body has come to rest. I could almost have dozed off.

The slopes below were dotted with black wattle and sisal. Beyond them the houses began, first the side streets that ran dead against the ridge and then the long avenues that streamed away to the east, dragging your eye through a wrack of rooftops and chimneys in the green foam of oaks and planes, all the way out to Kempton Park where the elephantine cooling towers of the Kelvin Power Station stood on the horizon.

Stunned by the sunlight, we slumped against the rock with our faces turned to the sky, while Auerbach spoke about the history of the valley and the people who had lived there as it passed from gentility to squalor and back again. You could still see some of the grand mansions on the opposite slope. Down in the dip, there were houses that went back to the beginnings of the city, that had survived the cycles of slum clearance and gentrification and renewed decline.

'You think it would simplify things, looking down from up here,' he went on, 'but it has the opposite effect on me. If I try to imagine the lives going on in all these houses, the domestic dramas, the family sagas, it seems impossibly complicated. How could you ever do justice to something so rich in detail? You couldn't do it in a novel, let alone a photograph.'

Brookes started as if something had bitten him. 'You were talking earlier about how you choose your subjects, or rather how they choose you. How does that work from up here?'

'It doesn't. There's no way of telling from here what's interesting.'

'Oh, I thought your point was that everything looks interesting from up here.'

'I said complicated, not interesting.'

'I'll say interesting then. That's what I think. Everyone has a story to tell.'

'But not everyone is a storyteller.'

'Fair enough. Everyone has a story, full stop. Someone else might have to tell it. That's where you come in.'

Brookes was fiddling a pen out of an inside pocket, as if he was thinking of writing this down.

'I'm not a storyteller,' Auerbach said. 'Even so, some stories are better than others.'

'Why?'

'They reveal something new. Or maybe they just confirm something important – or unimportant! They put something well. I don't know.'

'Now you're arguing my point. It's not the story at all, it's how you tell it. Even I know that and I'm just a bloody journalist.' He scrambled to his feet and teetered on the edge of a rock. A comet of pebbles was stuck to the back of the jacket where he'd been sitting on it. 'I'll bet you could find something worth photographing in every single house down there. Jesus, I'd love to know what's going on behind those doors. Can you imagine! You're the man for it, Saul! Pick one at random and let's see what it turns up. Throw a dart at the map.'

'That's exactly what some of my colleagues are doing these days,' Auerbach said, 'or it looks that way to me. Just point the camera out of the window and hope for the best.'

Brookes eased the strap of his own camera out of his collar and said, 'Why don't we test my idea? Seriously. Let's pick a house from up here, where one looks very much like another, and then go down and see what you can make of it.'

To my surprise, Auerbach jumped up rubbing his hands together, saying, 'Action, Gerry, action!' and the two of them riffled through the valley. After some joking about church spires and water towers, Brookes settled on a red-roofed house on our side of Kitchener Avenue.

'I'd better take a green one then,' Auerbach said, 'it's only fair,' and pointed further down into the valley, holding the pose until Brookes had squinted along his arm and approved the choice.

'And yours, Nev?'

Caught unawares.

'Come, come,' said Brookes, 'you mustn't be too careful, that would defeat the object. Eeny, meeny . . .'

In the game they had started, a miss was as good as a mile. 'I'll take the house next door to yours,' I said to Auerbach, 'the one with the orange tiles.' A glimpse of the roof was all you could see of it in the greenery.

'That's the spirit,' said Brookes.

Auerbach noted a couple of landmarks near the places we'd chosen, counting off the avenues north of Kitchener and the streets east or west of a steeple or a factory yard. Then we climbed into the Rambler and headed back down the koppie.

There was a lighter mood in the car now that we were setting off on an adventure. On safari, with Auerbach to cut the spoor.

In the back seat, with the window down, I worried about my choice and wished I could change it. The neighbours. The next best thing. It was meant to surprise, but it was dull.

We looked for the house with the red roof – 'Visitors first,' Auerbach had insisted. It did not take him long to find the place at the end of Emerald Street. He made a U-turn and drew up at the opposite kerb.

Brookes's choice was a city house with country manners. A corrugated-iron roof in need of paint beetled over a long stoep. On a balustrade with pillars shaped like pawns stood a fern in a rusty watering can and a birdcage made of bamboo, a Victorian replica by the look of it. A gate hung open across a faded red path.

'It's a student house,' I said.

'Watch out for tigers. They're not keen on cutting the lawn.'

'I was thinking of the curtains. Anti-Waste sells that cloth by the kilo. Every student place I know is full of it.' Linda had an entire wardrobe of dresses and pinafores cut from disfigured prints, factory rejects caused by a jammed roller or a spilt dye. When she sat on the sofa, you couldn't tell where she ended and the scatter cushions began.

'Let's see if anyone's home.'

'What will you say?' I asked.

'I'll think of something.'

The front door was framed by leaded panels, the regular pattern of blue and yellow spoilt by lozenges of clear glass where broken panes had been mended. Auerbach rang the bell. No one came. While we waited, Brookes strolled to the end of the stoep.

'What the hell!'

We all went around the corner.

At the side of the house, where a bougainvillea grow-ing on to the roof made a sort of arbour, a dozen skulls were fixed to the wall. Animal skulls, pale as driftwood, bleached to sea-shades against the powder-blue plaster. The centrepiece was obviously the skull of a horse. There were others whose shapes suggested the flesh in which they had once been embedded: a dog, a rabbit, and more I could only guess at – rat, lamb, lizard, mole. The way they were arranged, with the horse in the middle and the lesser creatures above and below, each in its proper station, the beaked birds under the rafters, the head of the dog at a height that invited you to scratch its ear although its jaw was dropped to snap at your ankle, made them seem less like trophies than ghosts, passing through the wall that instant, hungry for meat and grass, for air and company, breaking back into the realm of the living. One of the skulls had small, pointed horns, darkly whorled, as shiny as enamel. Suspended in the eye socket of the horse was a pocket watch with its hands hanging down, defeated.

'Is it an altar?' Brookes asked.

Auerbach snorted no.

To my fingertips, the bones felt slily manufactured. There were hard plates, smooth as china, and porous edges like baked goods, bread or biscuit.

'It's almost art,' Auerbach said, with his hands cupped to a windowpane and his voice fogging the glass.

I also looked into the room. The familiar mess of a student life: mattress, desk, bookshelves of bricks and boards, beanbag, coat hangers on a broomstick angled across a corner on the picture rails, clothes mainly on the floor. Here on the window sill, an overflowing ashtray and a candle, and something else, a bird perched on a branch, a mounted specimen like a display in a natural history museum. The creature in its natural habitat.

Brookes took a photograph of the skulls.

'Time stood still,' Auerbach said, leaning close to the face of the watch.

A path led down the other side of the house, blocked at the end by a wooden door. Just as Auerbach and I rounded the corner, the door swung open and a woman looked out. Whether she had heard the bell ringing in the house and the sound of our voices or just happened to be on her way to the front, I cannot be sure, but she recoiled at the sight of us and jerked the door shut.

Waving me back, like a game ranger concerned for the safety of his charge, Auerbach hastened towards the woman, greeting her in Afrikaans. She opened the door, a slight woman with an elfin face, and spoke to him through the gap. He pointed to the sky and then to Brookes, who had appeared at my side. She smiled uncertainly with downcast eyes and answered so softly her words did not carry to me. They spoke at length, with their heads inclined towards one another as if they were sharing a secret.

Then he waved us closer. 'This is Veronica. She lives here at the back with her husband, who's gone to work.' And he told her our names. Brookes stuck out his hand, but she didn't seem to recognize the gesture.

We all went into the backyard. It was cramped, cluttered, and garish in the sunshine. Facing us was the long side of a garage and the front of an outbuilding that was no more than a shack. Like the fences on either side, the corrugated-iron walls of the buildings were the colour of old scabs, as if they'd been sluiced with blood a long time ago. A washing line strung between two poles held some baby clothes and nappies, two bed sheets and a pink pleated skirt. There were thick pads of moss between the flagstones underfoot and lichens on the concrete doorstep. From a bucket under a tap came the yellow smell of soiled nappies and sucking sweets.

Veronica stood aside. What had he told her? Perhaps she thought we were officials of some kind: Brookes could have passed for a municipal inspector, especially now that he had taken out his notebook. What would she make of me, though, with my long hair and ragged jeans? I must spoil the picture. Then again, it hardly mattered whether she grasped what we were up to. Who we *were* was clear. We were white men. We would do as we pleased.

She was wearing a light summer dress and silver sandals with a wine-glass heel. You could see the bones of her face beneath the skin, the shape of her skull under her doek. In the jagged cage of the yard, with the air full of iron filings and rust, she looked out of place. Did she really hang up the washing in high heels?

I was embarrassed. On my own behalf, for being there; on hers, for being unable to prevent me. I remembered my father speaking to Paulina in the yard, how she always

came out of her room and pulled the door closed behind
her, drawing the only line she could.

For a moment, we hummed like a delicately balanced
mechanism with an experimental purpose, keeping the sun
in the sky overhead, let's say, or measuring the whiteness
of the linen hanging down like sheets of paper: Auerbach
with his hands on his hips, gazing into the doorway of
the shack, Brookes concealed behind the washing as if
he were a prompt in the wings, scribbling in his notebook, Veronica swaying gently, testing the blade of the
air against her skin. And me, looking on, standing by.
Much as I wanted to, I couldn't stop staring. Below her
left breast were three wooden clothes pegs with their
teeth in the fabric of her dress and they moved with her
like a shoal of fish.

A baby began to cry in the shack. Auerbach motioned
her to go to it. Then he spoke to her from the doorway again,
so softly I could not hear. When the baby had been hushed,
he half-closed the door and went to fetch his camera.

As soon as he was gone, Brookes stooped under the
washing line, thrashing through the sheets like a pan-
tomime ghost, and peered around the door. 'May I come
in?' His voice was a spill of white enamel on red brick. He
ducked his head and went inside.

I hung back, flustered by my own discomfort, repelled
by Brookes and the haze of deodorized sweat and proper
English that had begun to emanate from him.

The room felt even smaller inside than the view from outside suggested. Daylight, poking holes through the walls everywhere, drawing dotted lines along their seams, made the place seem temporary, like something you could tear up and scatter to the wind. Most of the space was taken up by an iron bed on which the woman sat, nursing two infants; what remained was occupied by two tea chests lined with blankets, which evidently served as cradles, and a third chest standing on end and holding a Primus stove, a candlestick, plates and mugs, a medicine bottle.

I know this because I have seen Auerbach's photograph. Probably you have seen it too and my description is redundant, or worse, inadequate.

Alone in the yard, I suddenly felt anxious. If the owner of the house were to come home now . . . a student might understand – perhaps it would be someone I knew. But even so, trespassing is trespassing. What would my father think if he could see me? He was such a stickler about the law and doing the right thing. A parking ticket threw him into a moral panic. He might still regret this little exercise.

When Auerbach came back with his camera bags, Brookes was wetting his handkerchief under the tap. He wiped the top of his head and watched Auerbach setting up the tripod, telescoping rods and tightening thumb nuts with the practice of a movie-screen assassin.

Going closer, Brookes said, 'That's one nil to me. You've found a subject. Not just Mother and Child but Mother and Children. Twins.'

'I'm afraid it's more interesting than that,' Auerbach said coldly. 'Or perhaps I should say complicated. There were triplets, but one of them died.'

'My God! That's terrible, Saul. You should have said something.'

'They were burning a brazier in the room to keep warm this past winter. It's a miracle the others didn't suffocate too.'

'Is that them?' Brookes asked. He was back in the doorway.

'It's the only picture of all three.'

'May I?'

It was unclear whose permission he was asking. He brought a snapshot out into the sunlight and studied it. 'Also a boy? This one who died?' Auerbach nodded. Brookes wrote in his notebook. Then he thrust the photograph at me, with an impatient grunt, as if to say, 'Here, see what you've done. Happy now?'

Veronica came out of the shack. She had taken off the doek and fluffed her hair into an astonished halo. She unpegged two woollen caps from the line – the pompomed caps you can see in Auerbach's photograph – took the snapshot from me and went back inside.

In a moment, Auerbach gathered the legs of the tripod into a sheaf and followed her.

A car door slammed in the street. Brookes did not seem to notice. He found a kitchen chair in the corner of the yard, sat down with the notebook resting on his knee, and went on writing. His head looked like an egg extruded from the glistening shell of his jacket. Once again, I had the sense that he was directing us. Not that he was writing down what we were doing, but that we were moving or standing still, turning left or right according to his design. Dialogue was no longer possible: all we could do was act. Respond to stage directions.

The photograph is one of Auerbach's best. Of course, it has a special significance for me because I was there when he took it, but it is singled out by the experts too. You can look it up on the internet. They say it embodies those apparently contradictory qualities you read about on the dust jackets of his books. The tender way the woman holds the babies, presenting them in their innocent perfection: her head is turned aside, as if to make it clear that the children are the subject of the photograph, but also showing the lovely line of her cheek and the hoop in her ear. The twins are identical, you really cannot tell them apart. The mere handfuls of their heads in the soft caps, lolling against her breast, make you fear for the slender stems of their necks. Their eyes are open, their fingers are curled, and for all their delicacy, they look vital and ready to grow. Behind the mother, over her turned shoulder, is the snapshot of the triplets, propped on a wooden crossbeam against the iron wall. It is possible to miss that picture-within-a-picture entirely, but once seen it looms larger, or you wish it would. It makes you bend your head to the paper, trying to get closer, although you know this distance cannot be altered. The depth of field is fixed, once and for all. The third child, the dead one, irreplaceably absent in Auerbach's photograph, persists in that smaller frame like an echo. But who can tell which child it is? The mother could say, perhaps, but she is absent too. In the circle of your eye, they all go on, living and dying, then and now.

Yes, the embarrassment I felt on her behalf was entirely misplaced.

Auerbach packed away his equipment and wrote their names in a notebook. He said he would bring her a copy of the photograph when it was printed. Again, he refused my offer of help with the bags. Brookes was waiting for us on the stoep, still writing, pausing between lines with his hand going up and down like a sewing-machine needle, as if he was covering the page with dots.

We had lunch at Raul's in Troye Street. The place was packed but Raul – the man who put the king back in kingklip – found a table for us in a corner near the bar. The atmosphere was oily and submarine. Aquarium light seeped from a tank where a little deep-sea diver, lead-soled boots sunk in drifts of gravel, opened and shut a treasure chest, over and over, spilling pieces of eight and an SOS in air bubbles. The fringes of seaweed waving in the depths were the colour of the kale in the caldo verde.

Brookes ordered the seafood platter for two and the waiter thought he was joking. But he was deadly serious, he said in a menacing way. 'I am *deadly* serious.' And he laughed like a mad scientist. He was always famished after a long flight. Who can eat that crap? A hijacker? And now a tough assignment on top of it all. While we were waiting for the food he moulted the jacket, at last, and tucked a serviette into his shirt collar. One after the other, he took four bread rolls from the wicker basket in the middle of the table, broke them in half and ate them. The waiter cleared away everything except the piripiri sauce to make space for the plates.

Then Brookes ate and talked and ate. He had filled up with questions again, and after a glass of wine they streamed out of him. He kept working the food into the pouches of his cheeks so that he could ask another one: Do the prawns still come from Lourenço Marques? Not Marx, mind you, Markesh. Is Frelimo maintaining the fisheries? How large are the regime's stockpiles of foodstuffs, fuel, ammunition? Is it true that the N1 was designed for troop carriers and armoured cars like Hitler's autobahns? Is Sasol running at full steam? Will there be another bombing? Are the Boors still in bed with the Israelis? Do they have an atom bomb? Are sanctions biting?

Auerbach said he only knew what he read in the papers, but he would do his best to answer. While he was speaking, Brookes peeled his prawns and licked his fingers, and scratched in his notebook, which lay open on the seat of the fourth chair, pinned by an ashtray.

Between mouthfuls, Brookes suddenly said, 'I can't get that woman out of my mind. What did you say to her? When we arrived, I mean.'

Auerbach was eating prawns too. He sucked the juice out of a head while he considered this question. 'I said I wanted to take her picture.'

'Oh, come on, don't be coy. I'm just interested to know why she let you in.'

'She wanted her picture taken.'

Brookes rubbed his fingertips with his thumb and drew a figure of eight on the table top. Formica with a pattern in it, almost a texture, like brawn.

'They always want their pictures taken,' Auerbach went on. 'Nine times out of ten. Believe me, it's the easy part.'

I was halfway through a sole, picking at its pale flesh, every mouthful bristling with bones. Another stupid choice. I should have had prawns too, it would have given me reason to splash butter and lemon juice, to suck at my teeth and burn the hell out of my mouth and leave a manly amount of wreckage on the plate. Instead I was sorting through this skinny fish, something a girlfriend would order. Usually prawns were too much like insects for my stomach: the piles of translucent shells and crumpled feelers reminded me of the beetle sediment that collected in the light shades in my parents' lounge. But I would have ordered them – especially had I known Brookes would insist on paying. Expenses, expenses, shovelling the proffered cash aside with the back of his credit card.

'What are the odds of giving birth to identical triplets, I wonder,' Brookes said.

'Must be pretty rare,' Auerbach said.

'You'd think the doctors would follow up on something like that.'

'That's the system for you, Gerry. The government spends the bulk of the health budget on whites. Meanwhile black babies are dying of gastro and pneumonia, Third World diseases, the kind caused by malnutrition, overcrowding –'

'Yes, I know all that, but I'm talking about the interest, the human interest. They've done something special. You'd think they'd have been in the papers, that they'd attract some attention, some sponsorship or other. A pharmaceutical company, a nappy supplier, Nestlé, something in that line. How is it possible that these poor people have just been left to get on with it? In a one-room shack.'

I pulled another bone from the corner of my mouth. On the ocean floor, the diver went on opening and shutting the treasure chest, while a dazed and sated guppy drifted out from behind some seagrass.

'Why didn't the people in the house help them? They could have run out an extension or given them a heater. That's what would happen in a normal society.'

'They're just students,' I said.

Brookes turned his magnified gaze on me. 'Then they should know better. They should be asking questions. It's the least you'd expect to develop at a bloody university – an enquiring mind.'

'It's complicated.'

'Complicated! You've infected him, Saul. What's so complicated about a bit of human decency?'

A slurry of sociology surfaced in me, more feeling than thought, a thickening of the blood. I felt myself redden, as if I'd taken a swig of the piripiri.

'Is there a more complacent creature than a white South African? You've mastered the art of self-deception. In a normal society, you wouldn't have a bunch of overfed students living like lords in a rambling house while a family of five squat in a shanty out the back. It's like Russia under the tsars. Students are supposed to go hungry, like artists, it helps them see things more clearly. It's a shed, for God's sake, it's no bigger than a fucking play house. The right sort of mortuary for a child.'

Brookes had hold of the table as if he meant to turn it over. Any moment now. Now. I saw the wicker basket in a swarm of breadcrumbs, the dirty roses of the serviettes, a wine glass and the fat speech bubble of grand

cru spilling from it, fishbone thatch, a fried egg moored
to the bloodshot eye of a plate by a crimson thread of
chilli, all of it afloat between heaven and earth, every
single thing thrown irrevocably out of order, beyond
retrieval but not quite ruined, yet. Suspended. Surprising though it was, the scene seemed familiar to me, as
if we had rehearsed the conversation before and could
only push on now to a foregone conclusion. 'What sort
of people are they?' Brookes would say with his leaded
boots in the debris. 'Are they empty inside, are they dead?'
The dead white interior resounded. But the plates were
still on the table top, the food was still on the plates.
Brookes was still on the other side of the table, which
was still unturned, with a maggot of rice on his chin,
waiting for my reply.

Repetition. Things had begun to double. There must
be a term for it. Is it a natural process or an historical
one? Should it be encouraged or suppressed? Or simply
endured? Perhaps every gesture will beget its twin, every
action find an echo, every insight become a catechism,
like some chain reaction that can never be halted. The
concatenated universe.

I found my ordinary voice. 'I've come across many student houses where there are people living in the servants'
quarters, and not just neat little nuclear families either,
uncles and aunts and cousins from the countryside. At least
they have a roof over their heads. It's not ideal, but you

can't expect a bunch of students who aren't even earning a living to look after ten people.'

'You mean every student commune has its own native village? What do they do for their keep – gather firewood? tend the cattle?'

In most of the houses I knew, the people 'at the back' brawled among themselves and the people 'in the house' insisted on keeping the peace. The intelligentsia, lightly dusted with Social Anthropology, confronting the lumpen-proletariat, thoroughly steeped in Late Harvest. I remembered Linda staunching a knife wound in a woman's back with a beach towel while I called for an ambulance that did not come (it was Friday night). In the end, we loaded her into Benjy's Beetle, wrapped in towels and a groundsheet from someone's hiking kit, and drove her to the hospital ourselves, and Linda talked to her the whole way to keep her conscious. The next day her husband, grateful and contrite, washed the cars in full and final settlement of their debt.

But I couldn't say any of this to Brookes. Every story I could tell to clarify my situation only confirmed the point he was making. The order we lived in was perverse. It could not be improved upon; it had to be overthrown. Kindness did not help. Guilt and responsibility were not the same thing.

Later, as we were rinsing our mouths out with bitter little coffees, Auerbach said, 'Veronica will find it easier to raise two children than three.'

Brookes's mouth turned down in clownish dismay, but before he could speak, Auerbach went on, 'That's what she said, anyway. Poor woman. I suppose it makes her feel better.'

The mask, the thing that could have been a scrap of rubber torn from a doll's head, was in fact a face. The other bits and pieces were easier to identify as human – a foot in a shoe, a hand with the fingers curled, intact. There was even a ring on the middle finger. The rest was meat and cotton waste.

He had not been run down by History or the Movement: he had been blown up by a bomb. He was planting a bomb outside a police station when it detonated prematurely and tore his body to pieces. There was nothing metaphorical about it. Thinking in metaphors is not always a good idea. It was Benjy who rebuked me for the habit one night when we'd both had one too many. 'You can call it an empty barrel if you like. You can say, "This conversation is an empty barrel." But what's the point? Why not just say what you mean? Maybe I'll get it then. Give me a sporting chance.'

I swallowed the sea water in the back of my mouth and leaned closer to the photograph. It was a cutting from a newspaper, covered in clear plastic like a school project and stuck to the wall above the urinal where you could not fail to see it, standing there with a soft target in your hand, your *manhood.* Alongside was a typed sheet – BE ON THE ALERT – explaining that it was my responsibility to keep my eyes open and report suspicious packages to the Manager, in brackets Raul. The man who took the snap out of the snapper. The picture seemed to me like the conclusion of an argument, the coup de grâce. But whose argument? Perhaps it was just a lesson in looking. I was too inclined to turn my head away, it was in my nature and my upbringing. I buttoned my fly and washed my hands at the basin. Then I went back to the cutting and made myself look at it squarely.

In search of the second house, the one he had pulled out of the hat on Langermann Kop, Auerbach drove us back to Bez Valley. Brookes made me sit in front as if it was a special treat, so that he could stretch out in the back with his eyes closed. Auerbach switched on the radio, although he did not need to tune me out. We were all distracted. The house in Emerald Street had proved the magnanimity of chance so fully it hardly seemed fair to test it again.

We rumbled down the long hot avenues.

There's the cover of his book! – I thought – it's that picture of Uncle Doug's, I swear. But I held my tongue. Just as there was no point anticipating a photograph Auerbach might still take, so there was no point recognizing one he had taken already. What could one say about it? Snap! And then?

He's playing a game – I thought this too – he's having some fun. All this wandering around the city is nothing less than a guided tour of the places he's captured on film. He's letting us know we're on his turf. There! That place with the palm tree! And what about that one covered in ivy? It was like counting caravans, Gypsy caravans like our own, when we drove down to the coast on holiday, a game my father dreamed up to keep me occupied when I got bored and restless. Who'll be the first to see the sea?

When we pulled up outside the house in Fourth Avenue, I had a more cynical thought: is this really the place he picked from up on the koppie? Neither Brookes nor I can contradict him. He might have chosen it this minute, relying on those intuitions he makes so much of. All you can say for certain is that the roof is green. Racing green. *Groendakkies*.

While Auerbach went to see if anyone was home, and Brookes got out of the car to stretch and peel the fabric of his shirt off his belly like dead skin, I strolled a little way along the pavement to look at the house next door. My choice. It was as long and narrow as one side of a semi, a place that had lost its better half. The half left behind was yellow. A dozen steps led up to a stoep with a metal railing of diamonds and quoits. Beside the gate was a letterbox with a pitched roof and a chimney standing on an iron plinth like a maquette of the larger structure: they matched one another perfectly, down to the orange tiles and the red door. I could not wait to see what was behind that door. It might take another man's charm to pass through it, but the choice was mine.

Then Auerbach came back to the car to fetch his bags and invite us in. This knack for getting people to open up surprised me less the second time round.

Mrs Ditton lumbered ahead of us down the passage, swaying at every step to sweep one thigh past another, almost brushing the walls. We followed her into the lounge. The room was lined with dressers and display cabinets, and for all its clutter peculiarly hushed and drained, like a little-visited annex in a museum. I remember stepping lightly from a patterned rug on to dark floorboards, aware that all around things were asleep on their shadows. Even Brookes took the boom out of his voice. Set out in cabinets of coffin wood and pillared glass were toby jugs and cruet sets, upturned port glasses, cut-glass dishes, fragile and flowery ornaments, iced frivolities for wedding cakes in lilac, rose and leaf green. Of course, you cannot see these shades in Auerbach's photograph, although the black and white is perfect for lacquered wood and tarnished mirror. The ball-and-claw suite is ankle-deep in shadow, the curtains are so densely grained they could be carved from the same heavy wood as the furniture. There is a murderer behind every one.

An object stood out in the gloom: a low coffee table with a cracked top.

'Is this from a lorry?' Brookes asked incredulously, shifting aside a pewter urn on a tea cloth. Now I also saw the table for what it was: a windscreen welded at each of its four corners to a shell casing.

'A hippo,' she said. The flesh of her arms shook with laughter.

'Military vehicle,' Auerbach glossed it for him, 'troop carrier.' After a glance at the table, he went back to rifling out the legs of the tripod.

'They drove over a landmine with Jimmy inside.'

'Jimmy?'

'My son.'

She watched Auerbach suspiciously. I saw that the pads of her bare feet were so thick and round that her toes did not touch the floor when she stood still. She seemed to be balancing on pontoons. Only her hair was stiff and angular, arriving swiftly at contradictory points below her ears. It looked like a hairstyle she had copied from Jackie Kennedy and forgotten to change.

'Was he killed?'

'No, thank God. I always say to him, Jimmy, God was watching your back. His mates had broken bones and stuff, but he walked away without a scratch. That's why they gave it to him when he klaared out.'

So this piece of scrap was a good luck charm. Or a medal.

I had a look around with Mrs Ditton at my shoulder. Jimmy's room was easy to spot: he had a Kawasaki poster on the door and Farrah Fawcett-Majors above the bed. The room smelt of fish. In the channel between the bed and the wall lay a clutter of flippers, tanks and masks crusted with sea sand, and a couple of wetsuits like bloated body parts. A speargun leaned against a wardrobe. Jimmy was a diver in Port Nolloth, his mother told me, but he'd been called up to the border again and so he'd brought his gear home. Couldn't leave it in Port Jolly, it would all be swiped. He loved the sea, she said, even as a baby you couldn't get him out of the water. Swimming before he could walk. It was a crying shame they wouldn't take him in the navy because of his feet.

Auerbach called her for the shot.

The main bedroom was as gloomy as the lounge. A pair of brogues, side by side under the bed, polished for a funeral. The suit they went with was on a round-shouldered dumb valet. Through a window, I saw the window of the house next door, almost close enough to touch and so perfectly aligned it might have been a reflection. I shifted aside the edge of a net curtain and saw that the window opposite had venetian blinds tilted against the outside world. I could not imagine what was going on in that room. Anything was possible. Everything.

Brookes was like a visitor in a museum whose point he cannot fathom. He stooped to look at objects on the lower shelves of the cabinets and ran his fingers over the embossed spines of a set of encyclopedias. He paused in the doorways of the rooms as if they were spanned by chains, leaning in for a better view. There must be something interesting here, his attitude suggested, perhaps it's hidden in the corner over there. In the kitchen, where the makings of a stew lay on a chopping board, he held a chunk of butternut up to the light as if looking for a flaw. Once he fanned himself with his notebook, but wrote nothing in it.

When I returned to the lounge, Auerbach had the focusing cloth over his head. For a moment, the darkness seemed to emanate from him, running out from under the stifling hood. Then the flow reversed and the cloth appeared to be soaking up the shadows that had lain there already. Mrs Ditton sat in the armchair beside the fireplace. The coffee table had been dragged away – there is no trace of it in the photograph – to expose the floorboards and a corner of the rug. Looming on the left is the largest of the cabinets, so imposing you would say it belongs in a department store. The chair has wooden arms with ledges for teacups and on each of these lies a pie-crust of crochet work and a coaster. The chair sprawls with its arms open wide and its fists clenched, and she wallows in its lap.

Auerbach shrugged off the cloth and stood beside the camera with the cable release in his hand. The shadows scuttled and settled again. He waited for something to happen. Or not happen. Something imperceptible to the rest of us had to become clear before he could release the shutter. Twice he stepped away from the camera and looked towards the door with a grimace, as if the situation pained him and he had made up his mind to leave. This caused her to look at the door enquiringly as if someone had just knocked.

I imagined the door opening, I imagined the room opening rather than the door, the door standing still while the house swung away on small hinges and closed into the eye of the camera with a bang. Patience, something is bound to happen. And if nothing does? That is unthinkable. We cannot be left here in this half-formed state.

While my thoughts were elsewhere, Auerbach took the picture. For only the second time that day, the shutter fell through the moment like a guillotine. You can see the relief on Mrs Ditton's face as she drops from the fulness of life into a smaller, diminished immortality. She looks grateful to have the air knocked out of her. Anticipating a paper-thin future, she floats free of the fat-thighed cushions and the sticky shadows, she levitates. It is there in the photograph, you have only to look.

For a moment after the picture was taken, she was reluctant to leave the chair. Captured and released in the same instant, she was unsure of her will. She had two destinies now. One of them she still occupied, the other had stepped away from her; it was receding into the past, but with its face turned to the future. She hovered in the chair, unblinking, afraid to move a muscle, as if stirring would smudge that other body in the camera and she needed to match it for as long as possible to preserve a resemblance.

For the first time since the game with the houses started, Auerbach's spirits sagged. Some charge had gone out of him and into the camera, which stood there primed and ticking. Still, I heard him laughing as he chatted to Mrs Ditton and wrote in his notebook. Where do you come from? All these years, hey? What's that Jimmy of yours up to? And *Mr* Ditton? Have you ever worked? Do you get a pension? With questions that opened into the rest of her life, into her complications, she was charmed back into the well-lit room of the present.

I went on to the stoep and fired up my old man's briar. Through the bay window, I had a new view of the lounge. Standing there alone, the camera looked like a detached observer, an expert on a fact-finding mission, with its chin up and its eye steady, drawing its own conclusions.

Auerbach entered the picture and began to dismantle the device, while Mrs Ditton floated on the edge of the frame. Now that it really was done, the pose abandoned once and for all, she wanted us out of the house, that was clear, she was like a woman hurrying her lover from her bed, urging him to be gone before her husband comes home from work. Her eye kept flicking over the shelves and table tops, dusting and adjusting, measuring the spaces between knick-knacks to assure herself that nothing had been taken.

Brookes came to perch beside me on the balustrade. Where had he been all this time? He had faded into the background like a song on the radio and now he became audible again, rolling his pen between his palms as if he was trying to start a fire.

'Well, I was right. That's two out of two.' When I gave no answer, he went on, 'Did you pick up some tips?'

'Sure, I've learned a bit about talking your way in. Perhaps I'll go into insurance.'

'It's been an eye-opener, I must say.'

'More like a door-opener.'

Next door there was no sign of life. The curtains were drawn, the rooms were dark. We would not be ringing that bell, I was sure of it now. When Brookes said he had an interview with a chap from MAWU, he had to get back to the King George – 'The place has international status, you know' – I was not disappointed. Nor that Auerbach agreed so readily. It had been a long day.

Nothing more was said about the third house. Two out of two is good enough. Perfect.

The car smelt of middle-aged men, of garlic, Brut and sweat, and thanks to me a whiff of pipe smoke, the finishing touch.

I asked to be dropped off in Hillbrow, I would fetch my car later, and Auerbach obliged by sweeping up Hadfield Road into Berea. He did not ask what I had made of the day. To be frank, I meant to avoid that question at all costs. Young people learn things intensely. They're impressionable, we say. The proper image is not a tabula rasa, we are not written upon or etched or branded, but moulded from a substance already dense with thought and feeling. Our teachers reach into us, skilfully or clumsily, it's the luck of the draw, and shape this substance, they make ridges there, hollows and curves, and perception runs over them, bending to the contours, breaking against the sharp edges repeatedly, until they are as familiar as the roof of your mouth to your tongue. Experience swirls through these channels like water over rock, being shaped in turn and given a new direction. The day had diverted a current in me, but I could neither express this change nor predict its issue. If I joked with Brookes about what I had learned, it was only because I found the lesson baffling.

In Kotze Street, near the High Point Centre, Auerbach pulled over. We all shook hands. Brookes gave me his business card and wished me luck in the profession. 'Remember to write things down – ' the door swung shut '– on an empty stomach!' They swerved out into the traffic.

I had said I was meeting a friend in the Café Zürich, but this was just an excuse. Even before the Rambler turned down Twist Street, I was walking. The streets were lit with purpose, the surge of energy released when people knock off from work, when they come out of offices and shops and the evening lies ahead. Every intersection, where the stream pooled impatiently waiting for the lights to change, was a small spectacle. Long strings of brake lights glowed like coals, exhaust fumes mingled with the smell of rosemary and roast chicken. I walked from one end of Hillbrow to the other. White boxes full of blunt objects turned over in my mind, thumping at every step. I drank a beer in Willie's Bar, I drank another on the balcony of the Chelsea Hotel. Pulsing with words and pictures, Exclusive Books drew me. Auerbach's book felt light in my hands. Perhaps his images, those dark things floating on milk, had finally sunk? I imagined that I opened the book and the pages were blank.

Long after dark, I walked over to Sabine's house in Honey Street and found her making supper, trying to turn the usual strange assortment of cut-price goods from the vegetable co-op into a casserole. She had a sackful of parsnips and runner beans. We sat at the kitchen table, with wine from a box in glasses filched from some exhibition opening, and peeled and chopped the vegetables. I meant to tell her about the day, but in the end I left it lying in the back of my mind, pressed to my memory by a pencil of light.

DEAD LETTERS

The end of apartheid put my nose out of joint, I must confess. Suddenly the South Africans were talking to one another. They wouldn't shut up. Every so often one of them would wave a fist or shout a slogan, but it did not stem the flow. The world looked on amazed that these former adversaries had come together to talk the future into a different shape. After a decade of wilfully excluding myself, I felt left out of the club.

I was reminded of the old line on wishy-washy liberalism (the adjective is stuck to the noun like a price tag). Black people, it is said, prefer a straight-shooting Afrikaner to a duplicitous Englishman. What sort of people are these 'English-speaking South Africans', how can you trust them when they don't even have a proper name for their *group*? You never know where you stand with an English liberal; but you can bet your life on a racist Afrikaner.

I had always been sceptical about this notion, but now I began to think it might be true. We are all caricatures, I decided. Let the houseboy unstrap his kneepads and the madam unbutton her mink, let the freedom fighter lay down his rusty machine gun and the piggy-eyed politician throw his fedora in the river. Who am I to judge them? They've taken the punch and now everything's working out for the best. As for me, the *hensopper* in the seven-league boots, there's really no excuse. I didn't go the distance. Looking on as the country became a symbol of hope – of all things – I couldn't help feeling I had squandered the chance to make my small bit of history.

For all that, I did not go home as soon as I might have. Apparently, I needed to go on excluding myself a little longer.

I voted at South Africa House. There was a carnival atmosphere, every newspaper would use the phrase afterwards. It's not often history steps down from its pedestal and comes to meet you in the street. Yes, we were making history too, I could see it that way if I squinted. So what if there were no proper ballot boxes, just bins with plastic liners? People did not want to leave afterwards. They lingered on the pavements around the embassy, greeting friends in the queue, laughing at faces masked in black, green and gold. I bumped into acquaintances I hadn't seen for years, even swapped phone numbers with a couple I knew from the anti-apartheid rallies way back when.

'We must keep in touch.'

'Ja, let's have a *dop*.'

Producing the old slang like an expired passport.

We became a tourist attraction. An open-top double-decker drew up and the tour guide spoke into her microphone. 'Over on the right, ladies and gentlemen, one of London's most enduring monuments, Nelson's column.' The cameras popped. 'And over on the left, one of its newest and most transient attractions: South Africans voting.'

It was a day for making and accepting gestures. I was embraced by strangers, fiercely, as if they meant to squeeze the breath out of the past caught between us, and I held on as if my life depended on it, to say this is not about *me*, this is *your* moment. All around us principles I had nearly forgotten, togetherness, solidarity, engagement, glittered in the spring air.

The broken shale of South African English, an abrupt concentration of flat vowels and sharp consonants, was reassuring and threatening all at once. I wondered what my own speech, worn smooth by ten years of English weather, would sound like to an African ear. If I went home – *if* – would my compatriots think I was a foreigner?

After I'd voted, I joined the tourists under Nelson's enduring column, where a babble of other tongues could wash the South African silt from my ears. Trafalgar Square has never appealed to me. I don't care for the excess of paving like pressed grey linen, it's too proper I think, a city square in a business suit. But on that day it had loosened its buttons. Even the pigeons, flung like scraps of paper over the roof of the National Portrait Gallery, seemed flightier than usual.

I watched the BBC reports on the elections in South Africa the following day, and the long queues of voters in the country districts, bent around thorn trees and thatched huts, looked like lines of print. My eye was drawn to the exclamation mark – the question mark? – of a white face. As the helicopter hovered to get these shots, some people looked up and waved like flood victims hoping to be rescued, while others flung jubilant fists into the air. Every face was turned to the future, but whether they were elated or proud or wary, I couldn't tell at this distance.

A few weeks later, my mother sent me a little corner-of-the-eye election story about an old woman at a voting station on the East Rand who had refused a ballot paper. Instead, before the surprised officials could stop her, she had thrown a handful of mealie pits into the ballot box. Chicken feed. She had been mistaken for a lunatic and arrested by the police, but she was a poet. Her gesture sowed nothing but questions. Who would squander their vote, this one in particular, to make a point? Had she used the ballot box as a granary or a rubbish bin? Or were the kernels meant to be planted? And if so, were they the seeds of hope or despair?

The poetry of the moment made me long for the prose of Johannesburg. I went to see a travel agent.

•

I rediscovered my home town in my father's car, the Mercedes he'd driven to work until a month before he died. It had been parked in the basement of my mother's flat for a few years. She didn't like driving it, she said, just fitting it into a parking bay was a mission. I promised to sell it for her as soon as I found something that suited me better, but then I had second thoughts. After a decade of using the tube, it felt good to be pampered. And it worked wonders on clients – it was a huge, glossy business card.

Then again, the car was expensive to run and reminded me constantly of my dad. The first time I drove it, which I had never done while he was alive, I felt him sitting next to me, a reluctant passenger, telling me to watch out and slow down and keep my eye on the road. He was so vividly present, I could smell him. Later I realized it was no illusion: his aftershave was still in the leather steering-wheel cover and the warmth of my own hands had drawn the scent out on the air.

The pressing need when I came back was to set up a business. I am a photographer, fairly independent, strictly commercial. I'd done a bit of everything in London, from catalogues for department stores to property portfolios, but I found my niche in the women's magazines. No high fashion, just run-of-the-mill advertisements and illustrations for features, those photos that say 'Re-enacted by models', the ones that go with a footnote that says 'Not their real names'. I was – am – the frozen moment guy. I specialize in things falling, spilling, flying apart. Before Photoshop there was some skill in this kind of thing.

Finding work in Johannesburg, going to every crappy shoot that came my way, took me all over the city. I got lost. There were offices and factories where I expected smallholdings or open veld. What had become of the aerodrome? The Snake Park? The new suburbs were not even in my father's dog-eared book of maps.

I couldn't stop driving: I had to see everything again. I went looking for my grandparents' house in Orange Grove. What I wanted to see was the front stoep, a long slab of polished cement like a pool of cold blood. I found the address but the house was gone, devoured by an overgrown double-storey that barely fitted on the stand.

One Sunday afternoon, I drove out to Bramley with Acker Bilk in the tape deck (the soundtrack of my father's life had turned up in a plastic case under the seat). My mother had warned me to expect some changes in the neighbourhood, but I was not prepared for Villa Veneto. The estate covered a dozen of the old suburban blocks. Matchbox houses for the middle class. I followed the wall to the corner where our house used to be and found the end of the driveway marked by the stump of an oak. The cross section was the size of a dinner table, you could have seated six people there for a country luncheon. Right on cue, the melancholy strains of 'Stranger on the Shore' rose like fragrant smoke from the grills in the dash. I drove on to the main entrance. It would have been easy enough to get past the storm trooper at the boom – another reason to keep the Merc – but the rows of tiled roofs and empty balconies were dispiriting.

I went back home.

On another weekend, I drove around Yeoville and Berea, looking for my old hang-outs down Minors and Yeo and Honey, wondering if any of them were still occupied by students. Everyone said Joburg was too expensive and unsafe for student communes now. More and more young people were living at home until they got married. A generation of Peter Pans. Their poor parents couldn't get rid of them.

A few months after I came home, I bumped into Sabine at the Rosebank Mall. We met on the escalators – I was going down to the movie houses and she was coming up – and we fumbled a greeting as we passed. Then I looked back and saw her waiting for me at the top, so I went up again and we had coffee at that place next to the information kiosk.

She'd been to some festival of apartheid films. '*Dry White Season*,' she said when I asked. 'I watched it on video once when it was still banned, but it was amazing to see it on the big screen. Especially now when the past is becoming visible in a new way.'

'You mean it's coming back to haunt us.'

'Well, not just that. It will heal us too, I hope.'

'It's a pity the past hasn't mastered a South African accent,' I said. 'Sgt Oddball wasn't up to it, as I recall.'

'They should have sacked the voice coach.' She gave the throaty, late-night laugh every man in her circle had found so seductive. 'He sounded like a Dutchman who's lived in Moscow for ten years.' While I was imagining this combination and wondering whether she was sending me up, making a point about my own accent, she spread the festival programme out on the table and showed me the other films she wanted to see, documentaries about the struggle and the history of African jazz, a couple of dramas that had just been unbanned.

She looked good. I'd told her so as she kissed me on both cheeks like a European, and I meant it. Her features had sharpened with age, the baby fat had melted away, and it suited her. Although she still wore her hair long, the hippie style was gone too, the baggy dresses of the Honey Street days replaced by designer jeans and stiletto heels. How old was she? I'd read somewhere that women look their best at thirty-two. Or they think so, anyway.

'What have you been up to?' I asked while she was sprinkling a sachet of sugar substitute through the foam on her cappuccino. I wanted to get in first.

'Where shall I start? . . . Name an era.'

The laugh was not as enticing as it had once been. Was she putting it on a bit? As I get older, I'm discovering how hard it is not to start playing yourself. 'What did you do after varsity?' I asked.

'I taught for a while, at King David Victory Park, of all places. I wasn't really qualified to do anything else with my BA.'

'Sure, Dad was right, it stands for Bugger All.'

'How *are* your parents?'

'My dad passed away a while ago. My mom's going strong.'

'I'm sorry to hear it – the first part I mean.'

Before she could take this further, I prompted her: 'And after the schoolteaching? I gather you moved on.'

'Fast. I had to do something meaningful, politically speaking, so I got involved in ELP, you know, the English Language Project. We were teaching teachers in the Vaal Triangle. It was quite something. We went into the townships a lot. This was during the state of emergency, remember.'

Actually, I didn't know and I didn't remember. The grainy footage on the editing screens in production offices where my work sometimes took me, and the scraps of news on the BBC that I watched with one eye, scarcely qualified as memories. You could say the worst years of apartheid passed me by.

'It must have been rough,' I said.

'It had its moments. The boere thought nothing of chasing kids into the classrooms. Some teachers kept a bucket of water in the corner in case teargas blew in through the windows. Ordinary people were so brave. To go on teaching in those circumstances – it was heroic.'

'You must have been brave too.'

'It's always easier with a white skin, you know, it's like a flak jacket. Of course, we weren't supposed to be in the townships at all. Once they had to smuggle me out of Evaton on the floor of someone's car, with a blanket over my head. Can you believe it? Me. Like a sack of potatoes. Playing hide-and-seek with the boere.'

She did it again: she gave the *boo* in boere a peculiar, ghostly inflection.

Later she'd worked for an NGO, researching and writing the new history that would be taught in the schools after liberation – 'We knew it would come!' – and still found time to get involved in worker education for the unions. I noticed that she used the word 'worker' mainly as an adjective – worker plays, worker poets, worker publications. Along the way she'd joined the UDF.

'I became radicalized,' she said with a snort. 'Imagine, we called ourselves radicals without a blush. It was appropriate too. If things hadn't changed when they did, I'd have gone underground. I was angry enough for armed struggle.'

'Each one teach one', 'Liberation before education', 'An injury to one is an injury to all'. The catchphrases were familiar, but I was sure they didn't mean the same thing to both of us. It felt like we were playing broken telephone.

'And you, Nev?' she said eventually. 'Where have you been hiding?'

'Well, you know I went to London to avoid the army.' It was the only flag I could wave to show that I also had principles. I told her about my brief career as a waiter, my lucky break in advertising. Probably I made it sound more trivial than it was. My self-deprecation irritated me, but I couldn't stop it. In those days (this is one of the lines I use too much) I was overly impressed by people like Sabine. I've learned to take their stories with a little paper sachet of salt. Now that it was safe to do so, every second person was joining the struggle, and backdating the membership form too. In retrospect, everyone had done their bit.

And who could blame them. Even the leading lights of apartheid, the men who had made and enforced the laws, were starting to come clean, not just recanting but voicing the doubts they claimed to have been harbouring all along. If the social engineers had never really *believed*, why should the fitters and turners keep the faith? Soon there would be no believers left.

People were not lying either: they were merely inventing. Perhaps the freight of the past had to be lightened if the flimsy walls of the new South Africa were not to buckle. How much past can the present bear? There was already talk of a Truth Commission. But people are constitutionally unmade for the truth. Good, reliable fictions, that's what the doctor ordered.

We did not talk about this. We talked about mutual friends.

Had I heard about Penny Levine? She'd gone swimming on Mykonos and simply disappeared. They never found the body, just a towel and a pair of sunglasses at the water's edge. Her mother thinks she's in the witness protection programme. Don't ask. And Geraldine, do you remember Geraldine de Gouveia with the motorbike? She bought a house in Coffee Bay. She was always a bit of a dropout. Benjy is still around, subbing on the *Weekly Mail*.

'You should give him a call,' she said, 'he'll be glad to hear from you.'

'Sure.'

'What are *you* doing now?'

'I'm taking photographs.'

'Really? I don't remember that.'

'A new interest. I sort of fell into it.' I told her about my little stagings for *Fairlady*.

'You must give me your card.' I could swear there was a sceptical undertone. 'Maybe I can make use of your services.'

'How so?'

'I've just gone out on my own,' she explained, foraging for the last of the foam with a long-handled spoon and then scratching through her bag for her purse. 'I was involved in voter education before the election. Remember Bob Heartfield?'

I did. He wore a ponytail before it was fashionable and always took his shirt off when we kicked a soccer ball around on the library lawns.

'He's my husband actually, and my business partner. We had this NGO teaching people about the electoral process, what a ballot box is, where to put the cross and so on. Now the election's out of the way, we've set up a small agency, my first cc. Educational development. The new government will be pouring resources into education. They need people to grease the wheels, brokers, middlemen, middle*persons*.'

This time the laugh really did grate on my nerves. I remembered Eich. It was Sabine who introduced me to him. Be sand, not oil. *Nein, schlaft nicht, während die Ordner der Welt geschäftig sind!* Don't sleep while the filing clerks of the world are busy!

I did not have a business card, but I wrote my number on the back of one of hers.

I was glad when she didn't call. Our friendly little chat unnerved me. It wasn't her really, it was me. I had failed a test, worse, I had flunked it deliberately, spoilt my vote.

I needed to get out more and Benjy was a phone call away. But what if the dog of the past woke up hungry? Let it lie.

Choices. I had misgivings to spare about Sabine's, but what about my own? Even as I tried to remake my life in Joburg,

I was preoccupied with the time ten years earlier when I had to find a place for myself in London. The more I tried to focus on the present, the more my questions dragged me back into the past. How do you know what you need when you're young and everything seems redeemable? How can you decide what to keep and what to let go if you have all the time in the world?

When I first got to England, I meant to stay informed about my homeland. I subscribed to newsletters, went to rallies, joined a march or two. I came across a war resisters' organization and put my name on their mailing list – I had left the country to avoid conscription, after all. In the booklets they sent, I saw the photos of dead guerrillas tied to the mudguards of troop carriers, and the white boys who all looked familiar, full of bravado under their Beetle Bailey helmets, and I counted myself lucky. I went to hear Dennis Brutus read his poems and marvelled that he was so much like a priest. I made a special trip to a shop in Hackney to get something for my bare walls, considered the posters of heads in the shape of Africa and fists clutching pens in the shape of spears, and came away instead with a length of Malian mudcloth to string across my bedroom window.

I couldn't keep it up. After a while, I started avoiding the news: when they showed another political documentary on television, another uprising, another funeral, I changed the channel. I'd had enough of apartheid to last me a lifetime. I hoped the system would collapse, of course, and I fretted over what might happen to my family and friends if it did, but I no longer felt responsible. History would have to get by without me.

The country kept its shape in my heart for one reason: my mother's letters. More precisely, her enclosures. Every now and then, between the carefully folded sheets of onion-skin paper, among brisk accounts of engagement parties and kitchen teas, there would be something else. A recipe for breyani, which I'd mentioned in my last letter. A Polaroid of Paulina at the wheel of my old Datsun, the hand-me-down car, on the day she got her driver's licence. A shopping list she'd found in the bottom of a basket at the Hypermarket: mealie meal, pilchards, sticky tape, Doom – with the last item crossed out. Occasionally, a cutting from the newspaper, some small story most people would have read past. These days the papers, even the serious ones, are awash with trivia, and there's nothing so strange it won't be syndicated. Back then, the ordinary oddities were harder to spot. It took a sensibility rather than a search engine.

This ragbag of fragments, collected over a decade, finally held me together. It became the jagged seam where the ill-fitting halves of my life touched. One evening, I was in Finsbury Park unpinning papers from the notice board above my desk and packing them in a Black Magic chocolate box, finally convinced I was going 'home'. And the next thing – it was months later, actually, but it felt like hours – I was in my new flat in Killarney with the box open on the kitchen table and the familiar scraps between my fingers. It was September 1994.

I leafed through the cuttings and cards with my feet on a three-bar heater – so much for the spring – and my head in two places. In two minds. Making this choice had not resolved a thing.

Sometimes photographs annihilate memory; they swallow the available light and cast everything around them into shadow. Two of Saul Auerbach's images were like shutters on my mind: Veronica in the yard in Emerald Street, Mrs Ditton in her lounge in Fourth Avenue. Dense with my own experience, but held there in suspension, in chemically altered form. If I could seize them for myself, my time and place would spurt like juice between my fingers. But how to reach through the frame?

The house next door was another matter. Over the years, with nothing in the world to measure it against, it had crumbled away in the folds of my brain, leaving a residue as evocative as the smell of my father's aftershave. It had the appeal of an incomplete gesture, always on the tip of my memory, just about to come back to me.

Living in Johannesburg again, I thought about the house next door more often. I was afraid to tamper with the memory – it was like a fragile manuscript it would be better not to touch – but eventually I went down into Bez

Valley. Auerbach territory: on every side, there were street corners and houses he had photographed, or might have, or would yet. He was around here somewhere, I knew, still doing his thing.

Mrs Ditton's house had disappeared behind a wall, an assortment of pillars, plaster and glass brick lumped together like a display of building materials. Given room to breathe, this wall might have suited a mansion, one of those elaborate new follies on the edge of the city; crammed into such a narrow space it could only look grandiose. It was all nouns. Through the tracery of a precast concrete rose, I saw Spanish bars on the windows, a prison gate on the front door.

The house next door – *my* house, the one I had chosen from the vast range of possibilities but could not enter – neither surprised nor disappointed. The instant I laid eyes on it, the faint traces in my memory were absorbed into its simple reality. The defensive touches were new: a doodle of barbed wire along the fence and armed response signs on the gateposts. Against the faded yellow plaster, the signs with their heraldic shields and pennants were as bright as stained glass. Rampant lions with flashy claws directed burglars towards Mrs Ditton's. The plastic numbers attached to the wall were spaced too widely, so that the place appeared to be counting under its breath.

As if the blinds of Auerbach's vision had fallen away, the day came back to me in a flash. I sat in the car, twisting the threads of my life in my fingers, while a young version of myself, a long-haired boy with a pipe between his teeth and his fists in his pockets, came and went on the pavement. My camera was in the boot, but I could not use it. A photographer! Sometimes the idea still made me quail. How on earth? When an acorn rebounded off the windscreen I took it as a sign that I was in the wrong place at the wrong time, and drove home to Killarney.

I arrived in London with no idea how to make a living. At least I had a roof over my head, half of a flat for which my father had paid three months' rent in advance. As unhappy as he was to see me leave the country, he'd done everything he could to help. My flatmate Richard was the son of one of his business connections.

Richard was an actor. The two of us worked together for a while in a restaurant near Covent Garden where the menu changed with the nationality of the chef. The word 'yuppie' had just been coined to describe our clientele: young people with money to spend on the finer things and no way of knowing what they were. Being a waiter was not for me. I would have been happier washing dishes if it wasn't for the tips. Orwell was right: restaurants bring out the worst in people. These days, we don't expect to be waited upon much, we're used to packing our own groceries and doing our own banking, but even then opportunities to be served were becoming rare. In restaurants, overpriced ones especially, people were flattered to think they had servants. Waiting on the lords and ladies of the realm knocked the last bit of working-class stuffing out of me.

Before I could give the manager a reason to fire the pair of us, Richard found me another job. One evening he asked, 'Can you drive?'

'Sure. But I'm not licensed for over here.'

'Probably won't matter. Can you use a camera?'

You did not need a licence for that. I went to work for John Hollier, a schoolfriend of Richard's who had a small production company. He talked up their documentaries for Channel 4, the hot new broadcaster, but their bread and butter was in advertising.

I was not qualified to be a location scout – I could hardly find my way to the office in Soho without a map – but it mattered less than I expected. My boss was an old hand called Alice and she did the research and made the appointments. Her briefings were peculiarly precise: she showed me pictures in back issues of the *Woman's Weekly*. Stuff the script. Then she would give me names and addresses, stick a business card between two pages of the *A to Z* and point me towards the tube station.

I couldn't remember the last time I'd used a camera. 'But it's the simplest thing in the world,' Richard said. 'You just look through the window and press the button. Make sure the client gets a sense of the place, the size of the room, the light from a window, some architectural detail they're keen on. Click and it's done. Send it off to be processed.'

It sounded easier than waiting on tables or painting road markings, but I was resistant. I kept thinking about my father's arrangement with Saul Auerbach and it made me feel like a well-behaved child.

The new South Africa was a bewildering place. For a while, I didn't know whether I was coming or going. The parenthetical age had dawned, the years of qualification and revision, when the old versions of things trailed behind the new ones in brackets, fading identities and spent meanings, dogging the footsteps of the present like poor relations. Sometimes the ghosts went ahead suddenly, as if the sun had reeled to the wrong horizon in a moment and left you following your own shadow down the street.

I remember shooting stills on one of those rainbow nation commercials where a cheerful circle of friends, representing all the major population groups, gathered around the braai to drink beer and braai chops (but not yet to hold hands). These nation-building epics brought a lump to my throat, even if the easy companionship among the cast did not extend to the crew. When I left the studio and went back into the street, the present felt like the past.

I also remember the first time I heard Penny Levine's northern suburbs drawl in the mouth of a cashier at Pick n Pay. A black kugel! She must have been to a Model C school (Sabine had told me all about it). I kept her talking. The papers were full of snide letters about the black voices we were beginning to hear on radio and television, and here was a girl whose accent could not be colour-coded. She struck me as a time traveller, someone who had gone into the future to show what was possible. The future is a foreign country too.

And then there were moments when the old South Africa reared its battered head. On a magazine shoot one day, I came face to face with the Great White Hope.

When Kallie Knoetze fought Denton Ruddock at Loftus Versveld in 1978, my father and I were in the crowd. Boxing was not my dad's thing, but some big wall-to-wall buyer had given him the tickets and he felt he should go. That night Knoetze extended a winning streak by knocking the Englishman out in the third. I never thought I would see the man again, but here he was, up close, head to head with a Datsun bakkie in a scrapyard in Benrose.

The set-up was simple. Bakkie with crumpled bonnet facing right, boxer with broken nose facing left, boxer poking out a glove – hooks, uppercuts, let him try them all and we'll see what works – as if he's just stopped the bakkie in its tracks. The client was a body shop. *When your car takes a beating, let us knock it back into shape.* Knoetze himself had been panel-beaten by an amateur. It was fifteen years since he'd been in the ring, but when he made a fist he still looked like a fighter.

The shoot was sticky. I asked him what his best punch was and he said it was the knockout. But once I'd soft-soaped him a bit – mentioning the bout at Loftus did the trick – he relaxed and started performing for the camera. The photo is in my portfolio somewhere. A high point.

Scouting. It sounded like bob-a-job week for the unemployable, one step up from the dole, and in London of all places. The idea made me sweat. If only I had the qualities that set people at ease – poise, charm, the gift of the gab. I was getting my hair cut in Camden Town and trimming my accent myself (I have always been a good mimic), but I was clearly a foreigner, a South African *nogal*, and toting a camera. As it turned out, though, there was not much to it. I discovered an aspect of the useful truth Saul Auerbach had revealed to me: everyone wants to be in the pictures.

We would all like to think, I suppose, that the confined spaces of our domestic lives are roomy enough to frame some greater drama. In the age of webcams and reality TV, the thrill of turning on the telly to find Joanna Lumley drinking a G&T in your sitting room, let alone a complete stranger eating Shredded Wheat at your kitchen counter, might seem quaint, but the impulse hasn't changed. We

have just learned to suspend our disbelief in more complicated ways. As much as we like to go behind the scenes,
we still want to be taken in. Once the movie has dazzled
us with its special effects, we want to see how it's done.
We're just as happy to see how it's done *before* we're taken
in. It makes the surrender to deception sweeter.

I was uncomfortable at first, poking around in people's
private spaces, but that soon gave way to amazed curiosity.
You cannot imagine the things I saw. Not the major oddities, those are imaginable – you know there are people who
rebuild vintage motorcycles in their living rooms or cannot
bear to throw away a newspaper – but the minor ones, the
colour schemes that made me ill, the collections of com-
memorative thimbles, the hallucinatory menageries of soft
animals. I took pictures just to prove I wasn't seeing things.

Little by little, I got the experience that should have
been required of me as a qualification, and I got the lie of
London too, in broad sweeps and primary colours. But the
moods of places are subtle; they can change from one step
to another, as Benjamin once pointed out, 'as though one
had unexpectedly cleared a low step on a flight of stairs'
(I have the quote here on my notice board). I learned the
basic English of the city, I followed the simple arguments of
avenues and squares, especially when they were underlined
by the river, but the things it was saying under its breath,
the cryptic conversations of unfashionable neighbourhoods
were always beyond me.

If the air seemed full of static, the fault was probably mine. I couldn't go down the Tottenham Court Road or Baker Street or pass through Seven Dials or a hundred other places without feeling that I was in a story. I was reminded of my first glimpse of England as the plane descended towards Heathrow and I saw the neat patches of fields inked with roads and hedges, the muddy ponds, closer and closer as the plane dropped, until I could see chimney pots and roof slates like paint swatches in autumn shades, and then a tractor going down a lane and the farmer at the wheel, and I slipped into the pages of a book.

The agency handling the Kallie Knoetze ad had offices in Bedfordview and I drove out there to show them the contact sheets. They could have sent a driver – you didn't email things in those days – but I was still relearning the map of the city and so I took them over myself. On my way home afterwards, I drove through Bez Valley. Against my better judgement, I went down Fourth Avenue again and stopped outside my house. The scene of the crime. The yellow walls were bilious in the afternoon light. There were two or three letters spindled in a wrought-iron curlicue on top of the gate. I collected the mail, climbed the steps and rang the bell.

I thought I heard a chime deep inside the house but no one came. I was just reaching through the security gate, meaning to knock on the frosted pane in the door, when it opened.

'Can I help you?'

It always irks me when someone starts a conversation as if they're behind the counter in a shop.

A small woman with a snail-shell of grey hair, more pewter than silver, lacquered and curled over a crunched nut of a face. Bespectacled. One of her eyes was made to look larger than the other by a thick lens. The big eye and the quizzical slant of the tortoiseshell frames made her appear unpleasantly surprised to see me.

'These are yours.' I thrust the letters through the bars and she took them without a word. She was dressed in black and wearing stockings without shoes. Good thing there was wall-to-wall on the floors, even if it was a dirty beige. In the pale dead ends of the stockings her toes looked like creatures suffocating.

I put on my nice open face. 'I was passing . . .' And that was the last truthful thing I said. For some reason, I began to lie. 'My name is Neville and I'm an historian.' Like a deadbeat at a support group. My mind ran on ahead. Or perhaps it would be more accurate to say that it looped back, returning to ground we've already covered, sniffing for clues. 'I'm writing a book.' I really cannot explain it. The reason I was on her doorstep – a visit to the neighbourhood years ago had made me curious about the house – would not have been hard to convey.

It would have been simpler than the story I was now concocting, that I had already made up in some way and kept half-formed in the back of my mind, ready to be filled out and flourished for the occasion. 'I'm writing a book about Rosco Dunn.'

When I said it, when the name staggered out from a neutral corner of my mind, I almost laughed and spoilt everything.

'The boxer,' I added by way of explanation.

The big eye was a wanderer. The smaller one stayed focused on my face. I tried to change my expression to one of earnest enquiry. *An* historian? I did not even have a pen. The subject of my book had stumbled into my imagination a few days earlier and my stop at the agency had reminded me of him. When he arrived for the shoot, Kallie Knoetze was wearing a red satin robe with 'Rosco Dunn' on the back of it and he wouldn't take it off. Our director had to call the casting agent and threaten to cancel the contract. By then she was on the verge of tears. 'You're supposed to be Kallie Knoetze,' she said, 'that's the whole point.'

'Who the hell is Rosco Dunn?' I'd asked the make-up artist. 'Someone he fought?' The name rang a bell.

'No, it's some character he played in a movie,' she said. 'A contender. You see the parallel?'

The snail-headed woman was in the dark too. 'What was the name again?' she said through the gate.

'Rosco Dunn. He used to live here. Well, not in this house, we can't be sure, but in this street. Do you mind if I take a look around? It would help my research.'

'In my house?'

I'd been back in Johannesburg long enough to know how suspicious people were. They always thought you were up to something – which I was. I should have told the truth. Except that telling the truth can make you sound like a chancer. In any event, the lies were tripping off my tongue.

'I'm trying to discover who he was, my subject, what he was like. You can tell a lot about a person from the place they grew up.'

'I suppose so. But the house has changed over the years. It won't help you much.'

'The details aren't important, I'm after the shape of things, the general atmosphere. It would help me a lot, I assure you, and I'll just be a minute.'

There were waxy runnels from the corners of her eyes to the corners of her small, pinched mouth, as if tears had dribbled and dried between the two. The big eye was settling down. Once that came into play, I was finished.

'People are very interested in Rosco Dunn,' I said, and again the name tickled me and I had to clench my jaw to stop from laughing. 'Even overseas. Someone is thinking of making a movie.'

The magic word did not cause the gate to spring open. In fact, she began to fade back into the dark hallway. I had to restrain myself from grabbing her sleeve through the bars.

'Perhaps I should speak to the neighbours instead,' I said. 'Do you know the Dittons?'

That reeled her in again. 'Oh no, you're too late for that. They moved away years ago.'

'Then you're my only hope, Mrs . . .' I should have looked at the name on the letter.

'Camilla.'

'Camilla. Perhaps I'll take a picture of the outside, if you don't mind, Camilla. I've got my camera in the car.'

My finger directed her lopsided gaze to the Mercedes on the other side of the street. Click. Her capitulation became audible in the sound of the latch.

'I suppose it won't harm.' She pushed the gate open. 'You'll have to excuse the mess. At my time of life, you don't expect visitors.'

When the door swung shut, the air shifted as if someone had clapped their hands together next to my ear. A lamp like an old ivory chessman stood on a table in the hall. Half-blind and blinking in the gloom, I followed her down the passage. The first two doors we passed stood ajar and the rooms appeared to be empty. The third door was closed. Looking back, she pressed a finger to her lips and said softly, 'Dr Pinheiro.'

The passage opened into a room I took to be the lounge, although the word did not fit. It seemed like a stage set, half-built or perhaps half-struck, and so sparsely furnished I could not help making an inventory. Under the window, an oak table and a straight-backed chair; in a row along one wall, five matching chairs pushed together to form a pew; at each end, a side table with a marble top the size of a dinner plate; on one of the tables, a brass bell; from a plain wooden pelmet, a fall of red velvet curtains; centre stage, like an island in a sea of beige, a small round red carpet.

I stood on the island. Camilla turned to face me, with her hands pinching a waist in the dress and her stockinged feet splayed, intent and suspicious, like an invigilator in an exam who has to make sure there is no cheating. Yet there was something girlish about the widow's weeds, as if she had put on her granddaughter's school uniform.

'I'll bet that was Rosco's room,' I said, looking towards the sealed door. His story was growing to fill the silence, sprouting branches and leaves on which I almost choked. I have never been a storyteller, but I found myself speaking in a new way, in a voice full of resonant echoes that seemed to come from a hollow space near me. 'On winter nights, he would creep into the kitchen to sleep beside the stove. Better a blanket on the floor than a mattress shared with two roughneck brothers.'

I had read this story in a newspaper. Certain details came back – the cracked heels of the brothers, the cursives of ash on his calves in the morning – but not the name of the hero. Who could it be? A politician probably. We were fascinated by the new political leaders, the activists and exiles from humble homesteads and obscure postings who held our future in their hands. Their lives read like fictions, these men and women who had organized strikes and smuggled weapons, who had studied soldiering or economics or medicine in places like East Germany and Bulgaria, who had been in exile or in jail and were now cabinet ministers and directors-general.

Rosco Dunn. The lie was like a time-lapse film. As I spoke, the scrawny, ash-grey child matured into a portly middle-aged man with an identikit face that took its black-rimmed glasses from Joe Slovo and its cowboy moustache from Kallie Knoetze. Something about this face reminded me of Gerald Brookes and made my stomach churn.

I noticed the corner of a handkerchief sticking out of Camilla's cuff like the ear of a small animal hidden up her sleeve.

'Would you like some tea?' she asked. And before I could refuse: 'How do you take it?'

'As it comes.'

'Milk, one sugar?'

'Fine.'

She vanished through a doorway. When I heard the water running, I went and looked through the velvet curtains. A garden had been left to grow wild there. The grass was so high that a table top appeared to be floating on it like a raft. Shrubbery frothed up on one side, a hedge of unpruned ivy was piled in thunderheads on the other. As I looked out, a ripple passed through the leafy pelt as if the garden had sensed my presence and shuddered. I thought I saw little houses in the foam, things that had been swept away in a flood, adrift but miraculously intact.

In the kitchen, cups rattled into saucers. Letting the curtain fall, I went and waited on the island. She came in drying her hands on a dishcloth and gave the room the once-over like a stage manager checking that the props are all in place. She had put on a pair of school shoes with thick rubber soles, and although they added an inch to her height they made her look smaller.

'Please sit,' she said from the doorway.

I sat at one end of the pew.

'History,' she said, pressing her palms together and raising them towards the ceiling. 'I suppose it keeps you busy. There's always something happening, isn't there.'

'It's one thing after another.'

'Good things, bad things.'

'Naturally.'

'What do you focus on?'

'We historians look at things from all sides. It isn't important if the glass is half-full or half-empty, what matters is how it got that way.'

'You don't have a speciality?'

'No.'

She seemed satisfied with that. She looked at the toe of her shoe. I puzzled over the meaning of the hand gesture. Was it an expression of gratitude?

'Except for boxing,' she said.

'Well, yes, you could say so.'

'What's boxing got to do with it?'

While I was trying to find an answer, the kettle whistled and she went back to the kitchen.

Dr Pinheiro. He seemed to be in quarantine. Something about that tight-lipped door said that it was closed on a sickroom. What was the matter with him? A disease of the mind, I imagined, or a sleeping sickness. I could feel the air pressing against the door, dream-stained, thick with make-believe, while he lay on his back on a camp bed with his striped pyjamas open to the waist, his hairy belly heaving, his nose sticking up like a skeg. Sweat ran down off his bald head. A tendril of vine reached in under the sash and groped for his pulse in the gloom.

Camilla came back with a tray. The teapot was in a knitted cosy shaped like a brooding hen.

'Dr Pinheiro . . .' I began, but she hushed me with a fluttered palm.

'We'll get to him later. I want to hear more about your boxer.'

She set the tray down on the table under the window, poured tea into two cups and offered me a shortbread finger from a plate in the shape of a vineleaf. Then she sat behind the table like a schoolteacher in front of the class.

At first, I did most of the talking. Bits and pieces of Rosco Dunn, cobbled together from boxing films and the sports pages, more or less convincingly rendered, and then scenes from my schooldays, less so. I told a story about being bullied that I'd heard from a drunken business journalist in the Ship one evening and connected that to the appeal of biography. Why I had become an historian, why Rosco had become a boxer. Stratagems banged around the truth like moths around an oil lamp. The whole exercise was soothing.

She refilled the teacups and began to speak. She told me how she had always wanted to travel, but never had the means. There were things she hoped to see before she died: the pyramids, the Edinburgh Tattoo, the Bridge of Sighs, the rainforests of the Amazon, the Panama Canal. She and Dr Pinheiro had marked their ports of call in an atlas with a dotted line that plunged off the edge of the Pacific near the Cook Islands, passed through many zones of darkness, and returned to the navigable world in the coastal waters of Fiji. Their Grand Tour! I gathered from the way she said 'Doctor Pinheiro', giving both elements equal emphasis, that he was the main author of their plans. Perhaps his illness had scuppered everything? I asked questions about the itinerary and made some comments about Cheops and Champollion to demonstrate my knowledge of history, but these interruptions made her impatient. She no longer needed me to speak, it was enough that I listen.

'Hercules van der Westhuizen,' she said, 'now there's a saga. Walking around in the same pair of shoes for more than fifty years! He bought them at a store in Oudtshoorn in 1937, he's worn them at least once a week ever since, and they've never been resoled. He says they've lasted so long because he polishes them after every outing, paying special attention to the seams.'

She paused and gazed at me unevenly. Did she expect me to tell a story in turn? I racked my brain, riffling through the Black Magic box of my memory, but nothing came to me.

'You know your sport,' she continued. 'Who is the greatest driver this country ever saw?'

Again nothing came. Should I mention my dad?

'Most people say Jody Scheckter, but I say Willie Nel! You can quote me on that. No man on earth ever drove further in one car in a single year. Between May 1989 and May 1990, he clocked nearly half a million kilometres on the freeways of the Transvaal in his Opel Monza. Up at three in the morning, on the road till late at night, six days a week. He couldn't have done it without his wife Rentia, who worked to pay for the petrol.'

It struck me that Willie Nel must have been driving – but where exactly? – when Nelson Mandela walked out of Victor Verster prison. I wanted to say something about this, to draw some meaningful parallels between Madiba's long walk and Willie's long drive, but as soon as I cleared my throat she patted me into silence and went on.

'Mrs Macfarlane of Edinburgh? No? She could teach this Hercules a thing or two about walking. She tramped from Land's End to John o' Groats in thirty-three days to raise money for brain research. What a story: she woke up one morning with a South African accent! Foreign accent syndrome is harder to deal with than aphasia, according to the experts, because the patient is regarded as a foreigner, and may even be treated like one by family and friends.'

I squirmed on the wooden chair. When I glanced at my watch, she took off her glasses and gave me a level look. Then she propped her elbows on the table, steepled her fingers and spoke more urgently, until the spit flew from her storytelling mouth. She spoke and spoke about driving and walking and talking in tongues. As hard as it had been to get into the house, it now seemed harder to get out again. Her voice changed and I lost the thread. After a while, I wasn't sure she was speaking English at all. I stopped trying to understand and simply followed the music.

The room faded to grey.

At last, like a man in a dream who feels the weight of the whole world on his shoulders, I struggled to my feet, and she fell silent. 'It's getting dark. If I don't take a photograph now, it will be too late.'

The car cheeped as if it were pleased to see me. With the tar tilting under my feet, I reeled across Fourth Avenue and got in behind the wheel. The sheepskin was a comfort. In this scented interior, where everything was soft and yielding, I felt that I had survived a trial. A car came down the avenue and its headlights picked out the old woman in the doorway, as tattered as a shadow, but still looking out for me. I should drive away now, I thought, it's too late for pictures anyway.

I went back over and spoke to her from the gate. 'We've lost the light,' I said. 'But I would like to get some photographs for my book. Do you mind if I come back?'

'Rosco Dunn! You've created a monster.'

We were sitting on the enclosed balcony of my mother's flat in Melrose. Usually, I saw her on Sunday afternoons, and we walked in the bird sanctuary or the botanical gardens and had tea under the trees, but in the hope of casting off the pall of my visit to Fourth Avenue I'd broken with routine and come to tell her about it. Her flat was as far from that airless Bez Valley lounge as you could get, its third-floor balcony a sunlit cabin caught in the crowns of plane trees. The old sofa from the house in Bramley was too big for the space, but we'd agreed not to replace it. What would a couple of leather armchairs set you back? The rubbish they advertised in the papers as if it came from Italy. Milano! my mother would say. The only people in Milan who would dream of buying such a thing are immigrants from Romania.

'Rosco Dunn and the Widow Pinheiro,' she went on. 'It's like something by one of those Latin Americans. How old is this woman?'

'I told you: old enough to be my grandmother . . . *your* grandmother. And she's not a widow, not yet.'

'She sounds quite glamorous in her own way.'

'Glamorous! She's an old crone. I've really given you the wrong impression.'

'What kind of man is the doctor?'

'No idea. We weren't introduced. He seems to be ill – although I can't be sure.'

'And what's the matter with you, telling all these lies?'

'I don't know. I'm quite truthful, generally, I think.'

'Your father and I brought you up that way. You must have learned to be devious in England. Why are you pretending to be someone else?'

'It just came over me. Something in the air.'

'What were you doing there in the first place?'

'It all started with Saul Auerbach's guided tour. Do you remember that?'

'You were still at school.'

'No, I was at university. In fact, it was after I dropped out.'

'Now I remember. Your father thought you needed vocational guidance and got it into his head that Saul was the man for the job.'

'I never told you how it worked out.' That was an understatement. My father had spoken to Auerbach about our day together, I gathered there had been a review of the lesson, but I refused to discuss it with him.

'You wouldn't speak about it, no, but you were in high spirits afterwards. He must have taught you something. He obviously inspired you to become a photographer.'

'It's not that simple, Mom.'

I told her about going up on Langermann Kop with Auerbach and Brookes; Veronica and the triplets, or rather the twins; the Portuguese restaurant in Troye Street, and everything else. Cast into words for the first time, that day came back in black and white, rendered more stark by the colourful lies of my meeting with Camilla. The time that had passed between my two visits to Fourth Avenue evaporated and the days fell together like photographs laid side by side on a light table.

My mother knew the photos of Veronica and Mrs Ditton. She had a copy of Auerbach's *Accidental Portraits* on the bookshelf in the lounge, which we could have consulted if we'd chosen. But it was Gerald Brookes she was interested in now. I must have given her the wrong impression of him too, and a compellingly unflattering one. What did he make of the day?

I had asked myself the same question when I began taking photographs in London.

Snooping around in the houses of strangers, English strangers, I was reminded of Brookes and my antipathy for him. So one day I went up to the library in Colindale to look for his article about Johannesburg and found it in the *Guardian*.

It was a long piece, a double-page spread illustrated with two or three of Auerbach's images. The portraits of Veronica and Mrs Ditton were not among them (he was famously slow to publish his work). There were also two snapshots taken by the author: a moody profile of Auerbach on the koppie with the industrial south of the city in the background, a wasteland of mine dumps and ravaged veld; and the skulls on the wall of the Emerald Street house.

The text was predictable. Brookes wrote about the abnormality of the everyday in a police state and drew a comparison between the leafy avenues of Houghton and the treeless shacklands of Alexandra. He had eaten the head of a sheep in an East Rand shebeen and a bucket of caviar at the Johannesburg Country Club. Wherever you turned, he said, there were shattering inequities in high contrast. Then he came to Emerald Street. I had been scrolling through the article on the microfilm reader, registering the phrases indifferently – Primus stove . . . rhinoceros-hide whip . . . Dimple Haig . . . here it comes . . . wishy-washy liberalism – but I suddenly felt exposed, as if the text were not on a small screen for my eyes only but projected on the wall where everyone in the reading room could see it. I skimmed ahead to see if my name was there, and then I cranked more slowly down the column, blushing with shame. This feeling returned as I told the story to my mother.

'Did he mention you?' she asked.

'Thank God no, not a word. He was too busy giving a frame-by-frame account of what Auerbach was up to. And describing Veronica, finding adjectives to apply to her face like make-up.'

'I feel sorry for that poor woman,' my mother said. 'Someone should have been looking after her. And the same goes for your Mrs Ditton, I feel sorry for her too.'

'Speaking of Auerbach, have you seen him lately?'

'Not since the funeral. We've lost touch. He was always your father's friend and your uncle Doug's, and I dare say your Auntie Ellen's, rather than mine.'

My uncle had been dead for years, but Auntie Ellen was going strong, and more prone than ever to hitting the sherry and the dance floor. This is what happens, the men die and the women can get on with things in peace. Now that my father was gone, as they say, my mother's habits had changed, along with the colour of her hair and the tone of her banter. He had been a meat and potatoes man, but she seldom cooked for herself any more.

'I thought you loved cooking.'

'Your father liked coming home to a plate of food, so I cooked.'

'You never really enjoyed it.'

'Up to a point. Anyway there's not much pleasure in cooking for one.'

I helped her put the deli on the table, the simple things

she liked now: a French loaf, smoked chicken, sweet-and-sour pickles, tomatoes. We sat down to eat.

For the first time in months, she spoke about my father's illness. It was the worst year of our lives. I would have come home to see them through it had I been able. It was clear that my father would not be travelling again. The false cheer when we spoke on the telephone could not hide the strain in their voices, each pained in its own way. The negotiations were going on in South Africa, but the place looked so violent from a distance. Everyone kept saying the process might still be derailed, it was not yet irreversible, to use the magic word. We spoke in riddles and I was never sure if we were talking about my father's cancer or the end of apartheid.

'He was so brave,' she said. 'Even at the end, he found it in himself to laugh. Once he sat down in his old camping chair on the patio and the canvas seat tore. How we laughed! – even though he was sick. In fact, that's what made it funny, that the chair should break although there was nothing left of him, he was skin and bone.'

Rosco Dunn was an echo chamber in which I kept hearing things. It was the perfect name for a boxer, not a champion mind you, but a contender. Finally I called Lenny Craven on the sports desk at the *Times* and he knew all about it. Knoetze had played Rosco Dunn in *Bomber* opposite Bud Spencer. *Skop, skiet en donder*, Lenny said, ham in all three disciplines. Rosco was a military man and the villain of the piece. I assumed the name was a screenwriter's invention, but when Lenny's fax came through I had to wonder if Knoetze hadn't made it up himself: Richard Dunn, Duane Bobick, Denton Ruddock. He'd beaten them all in successive fights. Roll the names together in your mouth and you might get Rosco Dunn.

My second visit to Mrs Pinheiro started badly. I had scarcely sat down at the end of the pew when she planted herself in front of the desk like a lawyer in a courtroom drama and said, 'You're not a historian.'

'Mrs Pinheiro –'

'You're much too young.'

'That's not important,' I managed to say.

'Why do you come with this nonsense about boxing? My father built this house. I was born and raised here.' She pointed a crooked finger at Dr Pinheiro's room. 'If there was a boxer in this house he would have been my brother, I can promise you that.'

'Rosco Dunn,' I said.

'Stop it, please. I know what you're up to.'

I was all ears.

'You're an estate agent.'

'Oh. Is that why you let me in?'

'I knew it! You get a feeling about someone. The minute I saw you, I thought you were in the market. This area has gone to the dogs and some stupid people are giving their houses away. You're not the first greedy agent to come snooping around here pretending to be looking for your cousin or collecting money for Boys Town.'

For a moment, my surprise that she was on to me obscured the fact that she was also entirely mistaken. It was tempting to go along with this new fiction, I felt like trying it on for size, but it was time to confess.

'You're right, I'm not an historian . . . but I'm not an estate agent either.'

She wouldn't listen. 'You work for Wanda Bollo?'

'Absolutely not.'

'Tony Braz?'

'No, I'm a photographer, a commercial photographer, and not a very good one.'

That stopped her dead. 'A *bad* photographer?'

'Scout's honour.'

'What do you want?'

'I was here more than ten years ago, not in your house but next door at the Dittons. I came with a photographer called Saul Auerbach, a real professional. We were going to knock on your door and ask whether we could take some pictures but we never got that far, we ran out of time. I never stopped wondering what this place was like inside. When I found myself in your neighbourhood last week, I decided to try my luck.'

'After all this time?'

'I'm sure it sounds strange, but it's the truth.'

'Then why didn't you just say so?'

'It seemed too complicated.'

With a disapproving click of her tongue, Mrs Pinheiro went to the sickroom, listened briefly at the door and slipped inside. As the door opened and shut, a tattered pennant of noise blew out through the gap. A moment later the door opened and shut again, and she was back with a photograph in a frame.

'Dottie left it to me when they moved,' she said. 'Something to remember her by.'

The frame was ornately leafy with the gilt chipped off its edges. Various photo-booth strips, creased passport photos and snapshots with pinked edges, tucked into the gap between glass and frame on either side, made it look like a stage with people peering out from the wings. Behind these rubbernecks, I saw Mrs Ditton in her lounge.

It was years before I came across Auerbach's book. Despite myself, I'd started taking more care over my photos. Using a camera nearly every day, watching people pick through my amateurish location snaps on the boardroom table – What on earth is *this*? – made me want to do better. Looking for guidance rather than inspiration, I turned to the photography shelves in the bookshops. On a Saturday morning, in the clutter of the Africa Centre, there it was: *Accidental*

Portraits. Ignoring the viewing copy on top of the pile of books, I bought one sealed in plastic, sight unseen, and carried it home like a guilty secret.

The photo of Veronica was near the front. As I paged, I had been picturing her in the yard, against the red iron walls and bright lines of washing, but of course she was inside the shack in black and white. For the first time I saw into the dim interior, where she sat on an iron bed cradling her two babies.

The caption read: 'Veronica Setshedi and her children, Joel and Amos, the surviving pair of a set of triplets, in their backyard shack in Emerald Street, Kensington, 1982. The third child, pictured in the smaller photograph, died the previous year from inhaling the poisonous fumes of a brazier. Veronica's husband Zeph is employed as a scooter driver by a large bank. They receive no special assistance from his employer or the state.'

My account of the day flickered in the glare of this image. So this is what will be left, I thought, for better or worse. This moment.

I paged further, through a long procession of Auerbach's people, municipal clerks, deep-level miners, shop assistants, a policeman with a cigarette pinched between his fingers, a flat cleaner with leather pads like shoes strapped to his knees, a house painter with freckles of PVA on his forearms. Absence had sharpened my relationship to these strangers. Without making the heart grow fonder, it had thinned the skin of my eye until every one of them could seem representative. In the flesh, on the same street, I would have kept my distance; at this scale, at this remove, they drew close and felt familiar. All their names were on the tip of my tongue. I kept thinking: I know this person. I know this kind of person.

And there was Mrs Ditton among her bruised artefacts, displayed like an idol on a cross-stitched cushion full of horsehair and gristle, her fingernails gaping like mouths.

When I turned the page, I almost expected to see the house next door.

Later I showed the book to Richard, thinking I might speak of my small part in it. He laughed as he leafed through it, smoothing the gloom out of every page with the flat of his hand. 'Can you believe these people? It's like Louisiana without the bayous. Son of a gun we're having fun anyway.' He was about to audition for some Sam Shepard play at the Tricycle – *True West*, I think it was, or *Buried Child* – and he said this was just what he needed for his research. 'Look at this moustache. Can you see me in one of those? I can use that.'

Richard's girlfriend Faith was less diplomatic. 'Ugly people in ugly places,' she said. 'The whites I mean. You must be relieved you've escaped from all this.'

'I'm sorry you're not an estate agent,' said Mrs Pinheiro, 'because I need to get out of here. Never mind seeing the world, I'd just like to see the other side of town. If I could get a room at Nazareth House, I'd be the happiest woman alive.'

She was behind the desk squinting at the photograph of Mrs Ditton. I thought of telling her how much it was worth: not exactly a pension, but more than pocket money. Now that South Africa had rejoined the global community, Auerbach's reputation was on the rise, he had become collectable. The experts were beginning to say that he was more than a photographer; that he was an artist.

'I'm sorry you're not a historian either. You could have written something about Dr Pinheiro. Such an interesting man.'

She tugged a photograph from the frame and held it out to me. It was a passport photo embossed with an arc of print like the inscription on a coin. A man with black hair swept back, a veined and bony forehead, and dark eyes gazing regretfully down a nose that was too long for his face. Not a bad likeness, I thought, less hair on the head, more flesh on the bones, a little less Bela Lugosi and a little more Marlon Brando, and he was the spitting image of the man I had imagined languishing in the room behind the door.

'I am not Mrs Pinheiro.' She left the words lying between us like the settlement of a debt. 'I may be the love of his life, but we never married. Sometimes I wonder whether there isn't a Mrs Pinheiro somewhere else, waiting for him in Mozambique or Portugal. People do not always tell the truth about who they are, as you know.'

Some people are born liars, I thought, and others acquire the skill through patient effort.

'Dr Pinheiro was a gifted physician,' she continued. 'He had a thriving medical practice in Lourenço Marques. He came down here after the Revolution, as they call their crazy carnival, with nothing but the clothes on his back. He was not the only one, of course, there were thousands of refugees like him, but he lost more than most, even his stethoscope.'

'How did you meet?'

'My brother found him at Our Lady of Lourdes and sent him to me. He arrived with a suitcase, and in it, a suit. That's all. I thought it was funny but he didn't see the joke. He was suffering. I took him in as a boarder, I had the room, and I let him stay for nothing until he got back on his feet. I could see he was a gentleman.

'He couldn't work as a doctor. They said his medical degree was invalid. There was an exam he could take and he was willing to study for it, he said, his English was improving every day, but the problem was that he couldn't speak Afrikaans. He got a job in the post office sorting letters. Can you imagine? A doctor, a man who should be giving injections and saving lives, standing all day throwing letters into pigeonholes. Sheltered employment for poor whites, for people with deaf ears and crooked feet. Yes, he used to say to me, it suits me, this job: I am a poor white.'

This must have been in the mid-70s, I thought, when I

was still a schoolboy. Where would the depot have been? Perhaps at the Jeppe Street Post Office. I tried to imagine the doctor there, poring over the addresses on letters and postcards as if they were secret codes, while I sat at my desk with the plans for a Flying Fortress spread out under the reading light and the picture of the finished model on the lid of the box standing on end like a screen. No matter how carefully I dabbed glue on the tiny parts, they ended up stuck to my fingers.

'Can you hear it?'

'What's that?'

'I thought you were listening to the voices. It gets so loud sometimes I can't hear myself think.' We listened. 'At first, it was just one or two, but lately it sounds like a crowd. Talk talk talk.'

The silence had a texture to it now, an undercurrent like a tap running in another room of the house.

'The doctor seems like a clever man,' I said. 'Did this job really suit him?'

'It was very hard for him. He didn't know the names of the big towns, never mind little villages or farms or railway junctions. Even the suburbs were new to him: how was he to know whether Troyeville was in Johannesburg or Pretoria or Blikkiesdorp? He had to learn everything from the beginning. It's a wonder he managed.

'Every sorter had a pigeonhole for letters that were not properly addressed or illegible. A few times a day, the Chief Sorter would go around the depot and collect all these letters, and then he would try to decipher them. In the beginning, Dr Pinheiro's pigeonhole for unsorted mail was fuller than everyone else's, and he worried that the Chief Sorter would notice and give him the sack. So he started to bring these letters home with him. He would have lost his job anyway if he'd been caught, but it was worth the risk. Together we went through the letters and I helped him decipher the addresses. It was like solving a crime. That's how we fell in love.'

Make-believe is easier to catch than truth-telling. I was beginning to hear things, a radio playing in a distant room or a dance party in the next block, a burst of laughter going up like a balloon slipping from a child's hand, and then an angry voice trying to talk over the others, insisting on something, making demands. And rushing beneath it all, so quietly it was almost imperceptible, an undercurrent of my own thoughts like a subterranean river under the house.

In the dark room, many mouths were working away at English, crunching it between their teeth and pushing it around with their tongues, grinding the edges off the parts of speech and breathing out the dust. Even the oldest words, the hardest and heaviest ones, could not hold their shape; sharp tongues peeled the patina off them like pencil shavings and revealed a green new meaning.

A single voice became audible. It was my old history teacher Prof Sherman, Hegemony Cricket himself, the most remarkable lecturer of his day, renowned for his clipped accounts of the migrant labour system and the rise of the African working class on the Rand. He had published five books with 'under apartheid' in their titles. I tried to follow his argument now, but all I heard was an insistent chiming. He was naming names. They fell from his lips, glittering and precise as newly minted coins, and sank away in the wishing well of talk.

'Where is your camera?'

'I beg your pardon?'

'When you came here, you said you wanted to take my picture.'

'I said I wanted to take a picture of the house.'

'Call me a liar. Even a bad photographer must have a camera.'

'It's in the car. I could fetch it, but I don't really like using it. It keeps a roof over my head, that's all. I suppose it's like Dr Pinheiro sorting letters.'

'You should find something else then. That's what the Doctor did. He moved on to bigger things.'

'Did he go back to medicine?'

'No, that was impossible. He worked for contractors, for builders and demolishers. He did the books. But he never forgot his years at the post office. It became a point of pride with him and also a bit of a laugh. He turned it into a sweet-and-sour joke at his own expense.

'One day, he came in with a letterbox shaped like a golf ball on a tee. I thought it was for my gate, but he set it up in the backyard. He'd salvaged it from some derelict semi they were tearing down in Bertrams, but he used to tell people it once belonged to Gary Player.

'When I asked him what it was for, he said it was the start of our museum. Somebody has to keep an eye on posterity. Before you know it, things have outlived their purpose. To the people of the future, letterboxes will be as interesting as penny-farthings are to us. He brought others over the years, gimmicky boxes shaped like shoes and dice, and many more that had nothing special about them, those common little rondavels and cabins with pitched roofs and a tube for the newspaper.

'It got funnier as he went along, but it was also serious. When we made a braai in the yard with our friends, he would tell stories about these things, where they were made and why they were special. He said the dice was a gift from Sol Kerzner. You never knew what he was making up and what was true. As I say, it's a pity you're not a historian. You could have separated the truth from the lies and written it down.'

'Well, I'd be happy to speak to him, if you like.'

'Not today,' she said with a weary smile.

'Is he ill?'

'He's gone.'

'To hospital?' And when she did not answer: 'To Portugal?'

'To paradise, I hope.'

'He's dead? When did he die?'

'A long time ago.'

'But I thought he was in this room!'

'I didn't want you to think I was alone,' she said, laying a scrawny hand on my arm. 'I'm very sorry.'

Some people believe in premonitions. In the popular wisdom, if you mistake a stranger for someone you know, you are bound to bump into that person soon. Mistaken identity is a kind of warning. I am not a believer. For a time after I came back to Johannesburg, I kept catching sight of people I thought were friends and acquaintances from my past, only to find I was mistaken. But I never bumped into the real person afterwards. It puzzled me that so many of the old crowd were gone. Some of them must have emigrated, others must be living in suburbs I never visited – the paths through the forest of the city do not all cross – and by the law of averages, a few might well be dead.

Then one day, without forewarning, I bumped into Benjy. We arranged to meet, and later that week we had a drink together at the Sunnyside. It was pleasant enough.

We spoke about our student days in Yeoville and he told me about his newspaper work. I gave him the brief version of my life abroad and we parted with a promise to get together again soon.

It was the time of the Rugby World Cup, which Benjy was following keenly. When he called to see whether I wanted to join him and his mates for the final, I felt obliged to go, although most of the tournament had passed me by. We watched the game on television in a marquee put up specially on the playing fields at the College of Education, a place I hadn't set foot in since Linda and I went there to build floats for the rag procession. It was a peculiar day. I drank too much beer and did my best to get involved, but my dislike for the game had only deepened since I'd last seen a Springbok team in action. Even when the Boks won, I was not as overjoyed as I might have been. The sight of Benjy and his mates, beers raised in clenched fists, tears streaming down their cheeks, while Nelson Mandela in his rugby jersey hoisted the trophy, will live with me for ever. A flanker. Who could have imagined such a thing?

The scale and intensity of the victory celebration took everyone by surprise. The city plunged into a delirious carnival of song and dance that went on all night. I ended up in Yeoville with Benjy's crowd, where a massive street party was going on. I drank more beer and did my best again. In Rockey Street, people were doing some sort of square dance and the sight of a huge troupe of strangers, hundreds strong, moving effortlessly to such complex choreography, was compelling. In a moment of weakness – or perhaps strength – I plunged into the formation. A woman took my hand and tried to steer me through the moves. It was a kindly act, one of many the day was blessed with, and I accepted it with all the grace I could muster. But I just couldn't get it. I was congenitally out of step.

When I brooded about it afterwards, I was reminded of an anti-apartheid march I went to in London. There was a picture in the *Independent* of the march passing down the Strand and I am in it, although I would have to show you which one is me. There I am, in the thick of the duffel-coated crowd, with my chin tucked between my lapels and a woollen cap pulled down over my ears. You would think I am trying to fool the photographers. All around me, people have linked arms with their neighbours, their comrades, but mine are pressed to my sides, I'm drifting along on my own. I am not a broken link, mind you, but I am a break in the chain.

My mother started writing to me again.

One Sunday, we went walking in the botanical gardens in Emmarentia. The rosebushes and the signboards in the Shakespeare garden with quotations from the Sonnets reminded me of England, and I mentioned how much I missed her letters. The enclosures especially, those snippets that turned a letter into a gift. Now and then, I would still come across a story in the newspaper and think, 'That's exactly the kind of thing she would have sent me.' I had clipped some of these items for my notice board, but they intrigued me less than her surprise packages.

A week later, I found a letter from my mother in my postbox. A note on airmail paper sent me greetings from Melrose and hoped that the weather and everything else was fine in Killarney. Folded into the sheet was a square of newsprint.

It told the story of a funeral at Avalon cemetery. A young woman was being buried and the mourners were gathered around the open grave at the end of a row of new mounds. Just as the priest gave the sign for the coffin to be lowered, a phone began to ring softly, as if from the bottom of a handbag or deep in a jacket pocket. Cellphones were less common then than they are now and the intrusion was jarring. The priest gave his flock an irritated look and a few people patted their pockets. The phone went on ringing. It dawned on them that it was coming from under the ground: the phone was ringing in the grave next door. There was a deathly silence, the report said, the mourners paused and held their breath, waiting to see whether someone would answer.

Photography-wise, Saul Auerbach's show at the Pollak was the high point of the post-apartheid period, according to the press release. It was not exactly a retrospective, because the selection favoured the contemporary, but it was certainly an overview, and a more reliable record of the past than any history book. Claudia Fischhoff had curated the exhibition along with the artist himself, tracing the development of various themes through his work. The reviewers liked it, although some of them thought there were too many buildings. 'Where are the people?' they asked.

What caught my eye was a notice in the *Mail & Guardian* to say that Auerbach would be doing a walkabout one Saturday afternoon. The man was known to be publicity-shy, which made this a rare opportunity for his audience to hear about the circumstances in which the photos had been taken and engage him about the issues they raised.

I got to the gallery early, so that I could look at the work myself before the guided tour. There were a great many photographs but arranged so sparely on the white walls that the gallery looked like a disassembled book. The detailed captions that were a feature of Auerbach's books had been stacked unobtrusively in the corners of the rooms where one was free to overlook them.

I scouted through the three rooms. Sixty prints or more, I guessed, arranged chronologically. In the middle room, a man was hunched like a dunce in a classroom corner, reading dutifully. To be honest, I was looking for the photos to which I felt a particular connection. The reviews had made me wonder whether the portraits would be represented at all, but I was not disappointed. Both Veronica and Mrs Ditton were there, along with some other images I always went back to in the books.

At the appointed time, I went to the foyer where Claudia Fischhoff stood with a sheaf of papers clasped to her chest. I gathered that her glasses, which disfigured her lovely face like one of those black bars for concealing someone's identity in a photograph, were a kind of disguise. She wanted to be taken more seriously than she supposed her looks allowed.

Auerbach sloped in through the emergency exit. A dozen heads turned in his direction. I was expecting an old soldier in boots and beret, but his baggy trousers and ill-fitting jacket made him look like an immigrant. If you'd passed him in the street, you might have thought he was a shopkeeper, the better sort of greengrocer. The art lovers, the fans were mainly women, I noticed. The men must be watching the Currie Cup on TV or making *potjies*. It was all the rage.

'Good afternoon people,' Claudia said. 'Please stand a bit closer. If you can take one of these and pass the rest on . . .' The stack of papers listing titles and prices went round the circle.

'Saul Auerbach needs no introduction,' she said. The man in question stood beside her, head down, shifting from one scuffed shoe to the other, like a schoolboy summoned before the class to recite some Tennyson. His face was flushed and his hair, which had thinned since our last meeting, stuck out at weird angles. He looked as if he'd been playing football with the security guards in the car park a minute ago.

Despite her opening line, Claudia proceeded to give an overview of Auerbach's career. While she was speaking, he fiddled with the fringes of his scarf and shrugged his arms inside the jacket, and glanced up from time to time to see whether we were still there. Claudia said that Auerbach was a great photographer, more than a photographer, an artist, a great artist, a colossus bestriding the frontier between photography and art, which had been portrayed as hostile territories too often in the past. After the facts and figures of his life – including his captaincy of the high-school cricket team – she swept through his early career, from his apprenticeship as a wedding photographer to his first documentary essays, which were notable for their gritty realism, she said, before turning to the major periods represented on the current exhibition in more detail. The thread that joined all these works, disparate as they might appear, she thought, was their honesty. The hand may have trembled, but the eye had never flinched.

And with that she thanked us for coming and gave the artist the floor.

Through all of this, Auerbach had been shrinking until the jacket appeared to fit him. At our applause, he started back into his ordinary size, thanked Claudia for her kind words and declared that he was not an artist. He was barely a photographer, he was still learning the craft. One of these days he hoped to take a really good photograph. He could feel that moment drawing closer. Then he thanked us for coming and suggested that we start where he had started, at the beginning. We trooped after him towards the 1950s.

Like many reluctant public speakers, Auerbach was articulate and engaging. Although he started out mumbling into his shirtfront, he grew more at ease with his audience photo by photo, and began to address us more directly. He had much to say about his work and its meaning, recalling places and people in great detail. Some of it smacked of the stage: you could tell that he had said it before. Disarmingly, though, the photos still surprised him, and despite having lived with them for decades, he seemed to discover new aspects of them even as he spoke. Once or twice, he stood staring at an image as if it had been made by someone else and smuggled in without his knowledge.

In every classroom, even one as informal as this, a few people dominate. We had an architect (I assumed) who spoke about the buildings in the photos as if the buildings themselves could speak – this one was glibly articulate, that one made a vertical statement, another declared its intentions in stone. Her language was so familiar to me – the world is speaking, things are mouthing off, they won't shut up for love or money – that for a moment she looked like someone

I knew. Besides this person, we had an earnest young woman who asked questions about the light and wrote the answers in a notebook. The only other man in the group, a pensioner with a startling pelt of ginger and white hair on his head and face and chest, hung back whenever we shuffled after Auerbach, leaned in close to some corner of the work we had finished discussing, until his horned eyebrows were nearly crumpled against the glass, and examined the surface minutely. The gesture reminded me of my optician zooming in with her penlight to shine a beam at my retina.

Would he recognize me? I had been wondering about this ever since I read the notice in the paper. It was half the reason I was here. I found myself pressing forward when the circle formed, foregrounding my face, dangling it there to be snapped. Of course, he had no reason to remember me; we had met just once and I had done nothing since then to distinguish myself. I had changed too, the long hair and the beard were gone, I was ten kilos heavier. But then the man was a photographer with a famously observant eye. I dangled my face hopefully, but there was no flicker of recognition.

We entered the second exhibition room. Another questioner joined the discussion. This particular image, she said, reminded her of Dorothea Lange's photographs of American workers in the Depression. What did he think of Lange's work? Was she an influence? Or should one rather look to the usual suspects like Walker Evans?

At last we got to the third room, where the accidental portraits hung. Veronica and Mrs Ditton were side by side on the far wall. We began to circulate in an anticlockwise direction. It was only now that I realized we had been going clockwise in the other rooms. Although the change was almost certainly insignificant, once it had struck me I couldn't put it out of my mind. It made some subtle difference to my orientation. I tried to figure out what it was, half-remembering something about the circulation of consumers in supermarkets and the optimal disposition of shelves, gondolas and fridges, but the discussion between Auerbach and the art lovers kept disrupting my thoughts. Out of the corner of my eye, I saw the ginger man, the one who reminded me of a raccoon although I have never actually seen such an animal, smelling a corner of one of the photos.

People were always complaining that he was overly concerned with buildings, Auerbach said, and insufficiently concerned with the people who lived in them. But in truth he had always been photographing both. If all his negatives were to be classified into those with people and those without, he was prepared to wager it would be an equal split. In any event, the distinction was immaterial, because people made the buildings and buildings shaped the people.

The architect said it was a classic chicken-and-egg situation, absolutely.

It seemed to me that this might be related to the distinction between clockwise and anticlockwise, but I couldn't think it through because the light specialist was asking another question. On the light, she said, and how he approached it: did he regard the light that struck a human cheekbone in the same way as the light that struck the side of a barn? Say.

The portrait of Veronica loomed. When we got there, I would introduce myself. 'You don't remember me, but I was there when you took this photograph . . .'

The furry ginger man slumped into a corner to examine the brickwork on a Dutch Reformed church.

We stopped at the portrait of a young girl playing the organ. Before Auerbach could say anything about it, a woman who had been quiet until then raised her hand, like a shy schoolgirl, and said, 'Mr Auerbach, I wonder if you remember me . . .?'

'You should have spoken to him anyway,' my mother said.

'I couldn't, the organist beat me to it. After that, I could only look like an imitator. Everyone made such a fuss – "I thought I knew the face!" "You haven't changed a bit!" – and she stood next to the photo so we could compare. Before and After.'

'You could have taken him aside,' she insisted, 'he'd have remembered you, especially if you'd mentioned Douglas. Your uncle was one of the first people to recognize his genius.'

We were sitting on the balcony at opposite ends of the overstuffed sofa. Her eyrie, she called it with a laugh, no self-respecting widow has a den. In the wintry light of late afternoon, with the branches of the planes etched against the glass and the distant rush of traffic on the motorway, it was like a tree house.

I told her about my last visit to Mrs Pinheiro and the Doctor's dead letters. The idea dismayed her. 'Dead *letters*,' she said. 'What usually happens to them, I wonder. Where do they go when they die?'

'Back to their Maker – if there's a return address.'

'And if not? There must be some that can't be deciphered.'

'They go round and round in the sorting room, it's a kind of purgatory for lost mail, according to Mrs Pinheiro. But eventually, with the authorization of the Chief Sorter, they're sent to the basement and they stay there in canvas bins for a year or so.'

'And then?'

'The incinerator.'

'Sounds terribly final.'

'That's what she said. That's why the hopeless cases, the ones they couldn't figure out between them, were never taken back.'

'He decided to save them! Pinheiro's ark.'

'Something like that. It wasn't legal, of course, but they didn't see it that way. The letters weren't stolen so much as borrowed, held in trust, she said. Apparently the Doctor always hoped someone would come for them one day.'

'And she showed you some of the survivors?'

'Yes, she went into Dr Pinheiro's room, which is closed to visitors, and came back with a bundle secured by two rubber bands.' Most of the letters were creased and soiled as if they'd been carried in a bra or a sweaty pocket, or dropped on a dusty pavement and stepped on, and the addresses reeled across the envelopes, sloping this way and that, or squashed together against one edge in an impatient queue. 'You could see these letters were sent by people who could barely write or afford the cost of the stamp. Half a person, half a place, bits of farms and villages, the name of a hill or a railway siding known only to the person who wrote it down. Names you'll never find on a map or in a directory.'

'It sounds sad.'

'It is. I keep thinking about what the letters must say, the good news and the bad, and about the people who wrote them and the people who never received them. Lost souls, calling after one another in the dark.'

I couldn't bring myself to say that Dr Pinheiro was gone.

The twilight deepened on the balcony.

'You should make friends your own age,' my mother said, 'you're spending too much time with old people. It's depressing, believe me, and it will make you old before your time. Leave Mr Auerbach alone.' After a moment she went on, and the lightly mocking tone darkened. 'I think you're looking for a mom and dad. The father part I can understand . . . but you've got a mother already. When you tell me about this old widow in her crumbling halls with her strange fancies, sitting around drinking tea and hearing voices, it's as if you're going off to an institution to visit some dilapidated version of me. It's a horrible prophecy.'

The door to the yard stood open. It was midwinter, but the garden was as lushly overgrown as ever, except that the grass had been cut to uncover a patch of brick paving on which stood a wire-mesh table and two chairs. A sickle lay on the table top like a gleaming question mark. I went into the garden and sat at the table with my coat collar turned up.

Mrs Pinheiro brought the tea tray and sat beside me. In broad daylight, the cosy was more parrot than hen. The letterboxes leaned out of the shrubbery like savages, glaring at us with cyclops eyes, or hung down shamefaced and glum, with their long lips pursed. The air was full of the radio static of insects scraping their legs against their bodies.

While the tea was drawing, Mrs Pinheiro slipped the rubber bands from a bundle of letters and fanned them out. In answer to the question posed by her enlarged eye, I tapped on one of the letters. She picked it up and tried to read the address. As she opened the flap the static broke off and a prison cell folded out of the silence, a small bare room with walls of the same pale green as the envelope. A man lay on his side in the far corner with his back turned to us. She folded him into an upright position against the wall and pressed a fingertip to his brow. He was shivering. With a sweep of her hand, she smoothed his damp, bloodied body out against the table and raised him to his feet. But as he held out his bound wrists and made to speak, she closed him between her palms like a paper lantern and slipped the letter back into the pack.

'Tea?' While she poured it for us, she asked, 'Do you like our museum?'

'I've never seen anything like it.'

'I thought you'd appreciate it. You should have seen it in its heyday, mind you. The Doctor used to cover the specimens with sacking in the winter, as if they were tropical plants, but I can't be bothered.'

We both laughed. To get the taste of leaf sap and fibre from my mouth, I reached for the biscuits on the tray. Eet-Sum-Mor shortbread in a box decorated with a plaid sash and a drawing of a baker in his apron. I noticed that he wore a collar and tie and had a pencil behind his ear, for taking orders or writing down recipes, I supposed. He reminded me of the Doctor in his passport photograph, trying to look blameless. Poor old Pinheiro. I imagined him lying in the sickroom with a postman's leather satchel over the back of a chair and the sacraments of a grim departure on the bedside table: Oros, cream crackers, a portable radio. On the wall, a motto in needlepoint: *Aluta continua!* Perhaps this was the photograph Auerbach was destined not to take?

'Let's talk about the letters,' I said, dipping a biscuit in my tea. 'Why have you kept them?'

'What else can I do?'

'But they don't belong to you.'

'But they do.'

Without another word, she unfolded a small girl into a shady corner of the garden. The poor scrap was barefoot and weeping. There was too much unhappiness in the world, I thought, in the world of letters, at least. Despite having resolved to stay out of it, I licked my finger and cleaned the corners of the child's eyes, while Mrs Pinheiro straightened her skirt and tucked in her blouse. She put the child aside and reached for an air letter. A man and a woman slipped out together in a fug of cigarette smoke and perfume, their limbs folded loosely into one another at the joints.

I tried to speak but my tongue was stuck to the roof of my mouth. My lips tasted of glue.

Mrs Pinheiro chose a padded envelope covered with stamps and opened it on the tip of the sickle. A paper chain of men and women, hundreds of them joined hand and foot, clattered out like galleys from a printing press. Between us, we folded them at the perforations, running the creases between our fingernails, and tore them apart. Free at last, stretching their limbs and cracking their joints, they began to tell their stories. When this envelope was empty, there were others, from which sprang an unbroken line of creatures delighted to suck air into their lungs and born to speak. All afternoon their numbers grew, until the air was so thick with stories it couldn't be breathed. Even then, Mrs Pinheiro went on opening envelopes in the fog and tossing the soft, damp forms into the crowd. I gathered the discarded pages, smoothed them flat and put them back in the envelopes. Mother's little helper.

Mrs Pinheiro walked me out. For some reason, I remembered that there had been a letterbox at the gate, a quaint maquette with a crooked chimney and windows of solder, and I asked after it.

'It was a model of the house,' she said. 'The Doctor's idea of a joke. It was made for him by one of his pals with a workshop. Pity it's been swiped.'

'Shall I take your picture now?' I asked.

'Why not? It's as good a day as any.'

I fetched my camera from the car. I think she was surprised that I really was a photographer after all. She wanted to pose in the garden, among the exhibits, but I'd had my fill of magic. I asked her to lean on the gate and that was that.

•

I came down with a fever. Flaring with light, leaking colour from the raw edges of my hands and feet, I lay in the bath until my temperature broke. At the worst, the water was boiling around me, frothing over the lip of the bath. Afterwards I felt overexposed and paper thin. The colour had been processed out of me. My hands were dusted with flour: I couldn't bear the pressure of one fingertip on another. My only wish was to be folded twice, put in an envelope and left undelivered among Dr Pinheiro's effects.

When at last I went in search of food and drink, I remembered how strange it was to come out of a matinee and find that it was still light outside, that the world was still there. The thrill of going astray between the real and the imaginary! We are in and out of malls so often these days we hardly notice the difference. The sun hurt my eyes and the discomfort reassured me that I would get well.

I stayed away from Fourth Avenue. My mother was right: it was unhealthy in a Latin American way.

Then one day I found a pamphlet about the postal system in my letterbox. Under apartheid, township dwellers and people in the rural areas had been denied access to mail services, the pamphlet said, many did not even have proper addresses. In the new dispensation, it was the aim of the Department of Posts and Telecommunications, as reflected in its mission statement, to rectify this situation, and thus play a small but vital part in building new communities of citizens and a new nation. A set of drawings showed the format of a typical letter, including the correct position for the address and return address, the stamp and the airmail sticker. A flow chart described the passage of a letter through the postal system, from the post office counter via the sorting depot to the receiver's letterbox. Another set of drawings with arrows and captions showed how you could make a letterbox for your front gate out of an empty paint tin.

The pamphlet spurred me into the darkroom to print up the photograph of Mrs Pinheiro at her gate, and I had it with me the next time I drove over to Fourth Avenue. But I did not get to see her again. There was a For Sale sign attached to the fence and no one answered when I knocked. The house appeared to be empty.

A few weeks later, on a Sunday morning when a show day had been advertised in the property pages, I went again to Fourth Avenue, half-expecting to find Mrs Pinheiro in attendance, but there was only an estate agent reading a decor magazine in the lounge. She had brought her own camping chair, an elaborate contraption with canvas pockets for magazines and drinks. The house felt like a different place. The floors were newly varnished – every last scrap of wall-to-wall was gone – and the walls were freshly painted.

'It needs a bit of TLC,' the agent said, following me down the passage, 'but it's the perfect starter home. You couldn't make a better investment. We're in rainbow nation territory here, the area is about to boom. People want houses near the city centre, well-built places with features, character homes. Have you seen the fireplace?'

Dr Pinheiro's door was open. Through the sash window I saw the window of the house next door, as clear as a mirror image. The room was large and clean, the walls were blindingly white, and panels of soft, perfectly normal light lay like bolts of silk on the pine floor. I stood in the doorway laughing.

SMALL TALK

'Are you the big grey wall?'

'That's me.'

'Then I'm here, Neville. I'm a bit early.'

'That's okay. I'll let you in.'

I put down the phone and went outside. When I opened the street door she was paying the taxi driver through the window. A younger, softer-looking woman than I'd pictured from her telephone voice, but dressed tough in cargo pants and a denim jacket with biker embroidery. Her backpack had a hard shell like a piece of body armour.

'You don't have a doorbell,' she said, as the pink Cabs for Women taxi made a U-turn and went back up Leicester Road.

'No, I had an intercom but it was swiped.'

'I scratched around there on the pillar, in case it was under the ivy, but then I thought, no, I'd better phone.' Holding up one of those thumb-and-pinkie telephones the comedians use.

'Good idea.'

'Oh, I'm Janie,' she said, as we went inside. 'Obviously.'

'Neville. I was just finishing breakfast. Would you like something? Coffee? It's Ethiopian I believe.'

'Juice would be nice.' She'd seen the split oranges next to the juicer. 'Before we do that though, would you mind letting me in again? I want to get something on my arrival.'

She unzipped a pocket on the bag and took out a digicam.

'I thought it was a print interview.'

'Ja, that's the idea, but I also need something for my blog. Just a clip, you know, to introduce you and direct people to the article. Nothing major. Do you mind?'

'I guess not.' I could already see her taking the camera out on a street corner in Bertrams. I didn't want to feel responsible for her. But the quip about introducing me hadn't gone over my head. On the strength of a single showing at an unfashionable gallery, and that in a group exhibition full of amateurs – not excluding myself – the *News* had sent a journalist to talk to me about my photos, someone who was prepared to spend time with me and do a piece with substance. A little fish in a full pond should count the crumbs.

I led her back down the path. She went into the street and I shut the door behind her.

'I'm going to ask you about the bell again,' she said through the door.

Shit. Five minutes and I'm already being asked to play myself. This whole thing is a bad idea.

She knocked. I opened. 'You don't have a doorbell,' she said. I explained the situation to the camera, saying 'nicked' instead of 'swiped', for some reason, and then we went back into the house. 'Nicked' is more nonchalant than 'swiped'. Perhaps I meant to suggest that the loss of my intercom was no big deal, I understood what drove people to petty theft, I was not such a bad guy.

While I was squeezing oranges, she shucked the jacket and looked around the kitchen. She did not seem old enough to be a journalist. But I am trying to resist the creeping fogeyishness that comes with middle age. Just because the economists on TV look like schoolchildren doesn't mean they don't know their onions, or whatever the vegetable measure of insight is these days. Portabellini mushrooms, if the markets are anything to go by.

'You're into cooking.' She was browsing along the shelf of cookery books in the dresser, making herself at home.

'I enjoy it, but Leora's the real foodie – that's my wife.'

'I'm very into cooking. I did a bit of an internship at Lemon Leaf in Stellenbosch. I see your wife's got their book here.'

'You can always get a job as a sous-chef if the journalism doesn't work out.'

I'd found the designation amusing ever since a client told me the sous-chef was the person in charge of gravy. The joke might have sounded merely mean, but she laughed and said, 'I'd like to have my own restaurant one day. The Lady of Shallot. You heard it here first.'

She tipped the Lemon Leaf book back into its slot and leaned over an old black-bound exercise book opened on a fretwork reading stand like a museum exhibit.

'That's more my style,' I said. 'I'm the one-pot specialist. You won't catch Leora cooking out of there.' It was a home-made cookery book, full of handwritten recipes and yellowed cuttings from newspapers and magazines, splashed with the ingredients listed in its pages, seasoned by use. 'It belonged to my mother. She gave it to me a couple of years ago when she stopped cooking for herself.'

'Some of these are ancient,' she said. 'Charlie's chicken marinade. My God, it's got condensed milk in it. Cheese straws. Rum baba. Lamb chops jubilee.'

'Half the recipes were passed on by someone after a dinner or a tea party or whatever. If you could piece it all together, you'd have a memoir. And a family tree.' I joined her as she leafed through the book, stopping occasionally to laugh at something – 'Baked Alaska!' – or look at the pictures. 'It's a bit of social anthropology too. The eating habits of the white middle class . . . under apartheid. You could make a study of it. Chuck-wagon chowder. That was a big favourite when I was a strapping lad of ten.'

'This must be your mom's handwriting, the copperplate.'

'One of the lasting benefits of a convent education.

Can you believe she learned to write with a dipping pen? She's a very precise woman. If it says 1 teaspoon of cinnamon, that's what you use, and if it's a flat teaspoon, you smooth off the excess with the back of a knife. She doesn't appreciate the theatrical style of cooking promoted by domestic goddesses and scooter drivers. A good glug of olive oil, slap it in the fuckin' mortar, bash it around a bit. What's that about?'

'Food hall hooliganism,' she said distractedly and went on paging. 'Do you actually use these?'

'I hardly need to: I've known a few of them by heart since I was a kid. But sometimes I look in the book anyway. The food tastes better when the ghosts adjust the seasoning.'

She sat down at the dinner table and unpacked the utensils for an interview from various zippered pockets: translucent pens with a skinny vein of ink in them like the thread in a thermometer, pinstriped erasers, for some reason a plastic ruler. Chattering away all the time. A trio of notebooks in the primary colours labelled in a tiny hand I couldn't read upside down.

'It would make a yummy cookery show. Celebrity sons and their not-so-famous mothers cook the family favourites. Fathers and daughters too, famous or not-so-famous or famous-until-teatime. With lots of wine between the paring and dicing so we learn all about their special relationship. Virtuoso demonstrations of the mezzaluna. Think Take Home Chef meets Prodigal Son.'

She was a talker. Good. It relieved me of the burden. Talk talk talk. And quick movements of her hands to put a word in quotes – 'celebrity' – or italicize an aside. Cheese straws? I don't *think* so.

I put the juice and a rack of toast on the table and sat down. She'd flipped the fruit bowl over to make a podium for her recorder, leaving the displaced apples and oranges arranged on the table top like a platitude. Good thing Leora was out. She was fussy about the bowl, which was the one acknowledged masterpiece from an otherwise undistinguished pottery class.

'Shall we start?'

'Please.'

'Cool. It's April the whatever 2009. This is Jane Amanpour reporting live from Somewhere Dangerous. Can you see me under this thing? No seriously, I'm with Neville Lister at his home in Kensington, Johannesburg. Just to fill you in, you're part of a work-in-progress series – we call it Riding Shotgun, not my idea – so I'd like to focus on what you're up to now. But seeing that people won't necessarily have heard of you, I thought we could start with some basic stuff about your background. I googled you but I didn't find much. You seem to have sprung to life in this group show at the Switch Box last year.'

'I'm a late starter.'

'Cool. Then you're ready to be discovered.'

She tweaked the recorder and looked at me through her fringe, which was styled to fall over her eyes without obscuring her vision. 'Fire away.'

I did the potted biog, including my misspent youth – 'Is it really possible to misspend your youth in Bramley?' – and my inglorious academic career. The London chapter came down to a line. When Leora reads a novel, she skips the boring descriptions and concentrates on the dialogue, and that's how I feel about my other life. I'd rather not go into detail.

'How long were you in exile?'

'No, no, that is a political fate I never had to suffer.'

'You left the country though.'

'I went away, yes, and after some time I came back again.'

'Why?'

'Why did I *leave*? To avoid the army and other unpleasantness. We had conscription then and I didn't feel like going to the border. The killing never appealed, to say nothing of the dying.'

'Did you think about becoming a conscientious objector?'

'For five minutes. I didn't have the stomach for it. Religious objectors like the Jehovah's Witnesses had a very rough time. Objecting on political grounds was practically unheard of. Once the ECC was formed it became more of an option, but that was after I left.'

'ECC?'

'End Conscription Campaign. Even with their support, I should tell you, you had to be a tough customer to make a stand. Most objectors just left.'

'What did you do in London?'

I told her how I worked as a waiter, not very patiently, until I fell into photography – 'without a splash.' I had been interviewed only once before in my life (for the Remarkable Residents series in the local knock-and-drop) and already I was repeating things I'd said then. Quoting myself. 'Out of the firing line into the frying pan.' For crying in a casserole. Give me a bit of time and I'd work the quotable quotes up into a routine.

She turned to the second half of her question: 'Why did you come back?'

'I wanted to be part of the new South Africa.'

Glib but true. In all the years I was away, I felt interrupted. Despite my resolve to look in the other direction, the life I might have been leading flickered in the corner of my eye. In another place, unfazed, a potential me was going about his business as if I'd never cut him short. Once apartheid fell – or *sat down*, as Leora likes to say – I could finally look squarely at this phantom who was living under my name. And then I got used to the idea that we could change places. A clean swap: your elsewhere for mine.

How I envy people who float around the world, resting their roots lightly on whatever soil they happen to be hovering above, dividing their time, and then dividing it again, until it's so thin they can see through it. The global citizens. Epiphytes.

Giving an account of my first years back home was harder. Grafting memory to experience had turned out to be painful. There was so much to be recovered, yet so little felt familiar, and the scraps that did had become resistant. A gap had opened up between me and the known world. When I approached the places and people I thought I knew, they took a step back, recoiling as if I meant to do them harm. It's no wonder I did not feel like touching a camera in the beginning. Nothing would keep still.

Eventually the world stopped fidgeting. The gap was still there but I gave up trying to bridge it, and then everything steadied itself sufficiently for me to get on with my life.

My explanation must have been even more evasive than I realized. She got the idea that I was talking about taking photographs, my 'process' as she put it.

'Are you a full-time artist?' she asked.

'I'm not an artist at all.'

'You've had photos on exhibition.'

'That's hardly a recommendation. Saul Auerbach is an artist. I'm just a photographer.'

'What do you do then?'

'Commercial work, movie stills and magazines, that sort of thing.'

While I was describing my latest product shoot, she opened the red notebook and leafed through it, and when

I paused she said, 'A new gig for Mr Frosty, quote unquote. I came across that in the *Viewfinder*. Why "Mr Frosty", if you don't mind me asking.'

'They're taking the mickey. The joke is that I'm known in the industry as the frozen moment guy. You know, the moment when things teeter, when they hover and vibrate, just before the fall. Capturing it in the real world is no longer a job for a photographer. Anyone can freeze an instant digitally and tinker with it and thaw it out again. You can take a slice of life and poke holes in it, change its colour, put bits in and take bits out until the cows come home. The results might be spectacular, but the magic is second-rate. We've all got the same smoke and mirrors.

'When it comes to these things, I'm like some old geezer who insists on writing with a pencil. I'm no Luddite, I appreciate the technology, it's just not for me. I still want to stage it all, to set up something foolishly complicated and get it on film, hoping for a small, unlikely miracle. It's a craft.'

'There's a demand?'

'Only because it's quaint. It's like french-polishing or . . .'

I went to fetch my magazine portfolio – my life's work – from the studio. When I came back she had the digicam rolling (in a manner of speaking) and she filmed me (ditto) making space on the table and opening the folder. Then she kindly dropped the camera in her bag and we paged through the pulls. What caught her eye, oddly enough, was a fashion series I did for Debenhams: the model's in loden green and chunky herringbone, according to the caption, perched in the bow of a Canadian canoe with her elbows on her knees, showing the camera a pouting mouth in which margarine wouldn't melt, while behind her a punter in a flat cap and a tweed jacket teeters over the water on the end of his oar like an overdressed pole-vaulter. The fall guy. In the next liquid moment, when this one unfreezes, there will be a splashdown. It was a long time ago, but I remember the job well: the canoe was supposed to be a punt, but what the hell, the budget was tight. I had to get the shot first time, because the stylist didn't have a spare suit of clothes.

The photographs I'd shown at the Switch Box, my corner of a group exhibition called *Public]/Private*, were of walls. Janie had seen them there and been struck, she said, by their chilly lack of judgement. She showed me a snap of her favourite on her cellphone – 'I hope you don't mind, it's just for reference' – a bleak suburban wall pierced by a loophole, through which you can see a grim warning notice beside a picture of a hooded cobra: 'Snake breeding facility – Trespassers beware!'

I laid out the full set of prints.

'What's with the walls?' she asked as we flipped through them.

I tried to explain my longing for the vanished city. As the walls go on rising, the character of the place grows more and more obscure. The mood of a street or suburb, that unlikely blend of outlooks expressed by the houses and the people living in them, no longer brushes off on you as you pass. You think there is life behind one guarded façade or another, a mind behind the blank stare, but you cannot be sure.

'It's creepy,' she said, 'I absolutely agree. It's like those people at Moyo who eat three courses without taking off their shades. You think they must be watching you, and so you watch them, which is the whole point.'

I take comfort in the debris strewn over the walls: the shadows of numbers pilfered for scrap, the unstrung lyres of electric fencing, the armed response signs, especially the old and weathered ones, which fade unevenly depending on how their colours stand up to the sun. Sometimes the names and numbers of the companies have bleached out entirely while the emblems of snarling dogs and charging elephants persist. All that remains on the oldest signs is two black pistols pointed at one another in a perpetual showdown. Their candour is admirable. They're empty gestures, like snapped wires and dog-eared spikes. The company faded away years ago, but their boards are still everywhere saying, 'Bang!'

I had photographed walls all over the city, some of them chanced upon during walks, others spotted from the car, focusing on the clutter, the faded threats, the scars of signs ripped from painted surfaces like sticking plasters. There was nobody to be seen in any of the photos except for one, which showed a woman beside a wooden door in a brick wall.

'And who is this?' Janie asked.

'That's Mrs Magwaza. She noticed me loitering with intent and came out to see what I wanted. She was the first of my thresholders.'

'Apparently it's good strategy for the interviewee to ask a couple of questions,' I said from the sink, where I was rinsing cups for coffee.

'Says who? Dr Phil?'

'I read it in *Business Report* actually, in one of those motivational columns. Best thing in the paper in my opinion. I guess they were talking about job interviews, but I'm sure it applies everywhere.'

'What's the idea?'

'Asking some questions of your own shows that you're curious, that you're interested in the world and other people, in a healthy way.'

'Your egotism has limits.'

'Exactly.'

There was a pause while I ground the beans and she read about the Ethiopian coffee-drinking ceremony on the package. Then she said, 'Ready when you are.'

'Do you like your job?'

'Some of it. It's quite varied, mostly interviews, personality pieces or profiles like this one. I don't really do straight features. And then I've got a blog where I review exhibitions and concerts, as well as art and design books, interior design and landscaping, collectables, coffee-table stuff. It's a great way to build up a library.

'On the blog I also offer household hints, taking stains out of carpets, dyeing cottons with indigenous herbal teas, mixing your own environmentally friendly air-fresheners. And then stuff like how to make a snow cave and survive if you're buried under an avalanche or why everyone should carry a surgical glove and a clove in the cubbyhole. The whole blog has this dualism. It's like the Book of the Week meets Reuben the Screwman.'

A happy meeting, I thought. I said, 'That's incredible.'

'It's my thing, it's what I'm known for.'

I was grinning, but she went on, 'I've got the best advice. The tips are definitive.'

'For example . . .'

'Well.' She scraped some orange pulp off the rim of the glass on her finger and put it in her mouth. 'Okay. You know how frustrating it is to get the price tags off things? They make them extra sticky so that shoplifters can't switch them around. They don't care what happens when you get the thing home. Some people couldn't be bothered. Ten years later, the bathroom scale's still got the bar code stuck to it. Other people can't wait to get rid of them and every last smear of glue must go, even if they have to swab it off with benzine, it's like a sign that they've taken possession. I'm sort of in-between, it depends on the object. If it's cheap and nasty, I don't really mind. Anyway, here's the tip: if you wave the flame of a cigarette lighter over the tag for a few seconds, it will peel off just like *that*.' A castanet click of the fingers. 'Of course, you've got to be careful when you're playing with fire. It works perfectly on glass, I promise, there's no need to kill yourself scratching the price off a bottle of wine. It works on books too. Just watch you don't set the merchandise alight.'

'That's amazing.' I meant it.

'I can get merlot out of a white linen sofa like *that*' – splitting another second between thumb and middle finger – 'but I won't bore you with the details.'

'And then you also write criticism about art and music.'

'Ja.'

'Are you serious?'

'Well, it's meant to be funny, obviously. Give me some credit, Neville. I know the difference between a household hint and an oratorio by Handel. It's a branding thing, it gives me the edge on my competitors, and readers find the mix amusing. But the hints work, believe me, I test them all myself. It's a question of credibility. Without that, everything would fall apart.'

•

181

'Saul Auerbach,' she said, 'he was the reason you became a photographer.'

'No, we can't blame him for that.'

'But he influenced you.'

I let the statement settle while I drove the plunger down to the bottom of the cafetière.

'My uncle had a photograph by Auerbach in his house when I was a kid. You would recognize it, I'm sure, a street corner in Judith's Paarl. It really bothered me. I couldn't see the point of having it on the wall. Then in my student days my father gave me a copy of Auerbach's first book and that was my real introduction to his work. To be honest, it was disturbing to see my own world presented so coldly. For the first time, the houses I lived in, the people I passed in the street were at the right distance to be grasped fully. They looked so solid, they were so *there*, I felt I knew them all. And yet there was a levity to them as well, because a photograph is a flimsy thing when you compare it to the world. It's always on the verge of floating away or turning to ashes. You don't want to go waving a lighter in that vicinity.

'But I'm speculating. I might be making it up. I *must* be making some of it up, because I can only imagine what I saw when I first looked at an Auerbach. They've been stored in the darkroom of my memory for too long, reproduced a hundred times for a hundred different reasons, packed away again under the tissue-paper layers of living, and I'm not sure at all what they revealed to my young self.'

Apparently a personality could get away with phrases like 'the darkroom of memory' or 'tissue-paper layers of living' if the delivery was natural enough.

'Did you ever meet?'

A direct question. I'd meant to avoid the subject, but now I told her about my day with Auerbach and Brookes. The gist of it anyway. Although the experience had made a more decisive impression on me than the photographs themselves, I had seldom spoken about it and the details had been slipping away. The last time Leora and I discussed my initiation, as she calls it, I had the feeling I was embellishing, adding in touches I couldn't possibly have remembered. These days, when I think about that time, Auerbach's accidental portraits come into my mind and they seem more reliable than my own memories.

Janie was curious about Auerbach's legendary impatience with people and patience with light. Is it true, she wanted to know, that he'll wait all day for a shadow to lengthen?

I answered as well as I could and she wrote in the green notebook. I wondered what she was writing down that she could not retrieve from the recorder.

The gist. It's always the gist, isn't it? We're left with so little to go on. Only the present is full enough to seem complete, and even that is an optical illusion. The moment is bleeding off the page. We live on the precipice of our perceptions. At the edge of every living instant, the world shears away like a cliff of ice into the sea of what is forgotten.

Mrs Magwaza was my first thresholder. Despite an apparently impenetrable wall, she had spotted me outside her house. Perhaps a neighbour with a clear view of the street had called to alert her to my suspicious presence. She came out and challenged me as I was setting up the tripod on the opposite kerb. Once I'd explained, she was happy enough to pose, although I had to dissuade her from going inside first to change into her Sunday best.

In the photo, she is holding my dissuasion in her left hand, a small consideration, which I'd been carrying in the cubbyhole for this very purpose. If not for the way she presents the envelope to the camera, suggesting that it's more important than this, you might think it is a letter she has just retrieved from the box in the wall beside her. In her housecoat and slippers, she looks like an office cleaner accepting a long-service award or a lucky shopper who has just won a voucher in a raffle at the supermarket.

Mrs Magwaza gave me faith in the human subject. I admired the way she stood between me and her privacy like an amiable security guard. I was moved.

'Weren't you curious to go inside,' Janie asked, 'to see how she lives?'

'Not at all.'

'I really want to see behind the wall.'

'I don't. Just thinking about the interior makes me squirm.'

I showed her the pictures that had followed: Mr Passmore of Dowerglen at his curly wrought-iron gate. On the wall of prefab cement panels is one of those increasingly rare signs that says 'Beware of the Dog! Pasop vir die Hond!' The letterbox is an alpine chalet with a slate roof. Then old Mrs Spoerk with her nursery rhyme box in the shape of a boot, a fibreglass novelty from the '60s that Dr Pinheiro would have given his eye teeth for.

These were the photos Claudia Fischhoff had come to see a few months ago. Out of the blue, she had called to say she was curating a show for the Pollak and thought my project might fit the bill. 'Project' was too grand a term, but I was flattered. Presumably Claudia's interest had fuelled Janie's. But what had prompted Claudia's? I had no idea. One hand was washing the other, scratching the reciprocal itch, doing what hands apparently do in the wonderful world of appearances.

I had taken half a dozen portraits of people at their gates before I noticed that every one of them included a letterbox. I pointed it out to Janie as we leafed through the prints.

'I've got it into my head that the people look like their letterboxes. What do you think? It's like people and their dogs. Have you ever been to a dog show? The resemblances are uncanny. The chap with the St Bernard always has a mop of curls and a shaggy beard. The elegant anorexics have borzois. Retired ballerinas, I'm sure. There are unwritten rules at play. Take a look at Roelof here with his browbeaten letterbox. Have you ever seen such an unhappy-looking man? It's like he's been cemented into a wall himself.'

I pulled the Charade out of the garage (quite right, I bought it for the name) and we went down into Bez Valley. She didn't drive at all, Janie said. When I asked why not, she said she was ahead of the game, preparing for the day we ran out of gas, collectively. I took this as a criticism. She was growing her own vegetables too and generating her own electricity.

On the drive, her phone sneezed twice to attract attention. The conversations were quick and cryptic. Hey. Cool. You wish. She sent two rapid-fire text messages. Between calls, she took photos with her left hand, reaching out of the window with a small silver camera as if she were tapping ash off a cigarette.

'You're busy,' I said.

'Popular,' she corrected me. 'I'm quite famous, you know. I've been on the cover of *Lifestyle*. I'm my own wallpaper.' Holding up the phone for me to see.

I'd spoken to Hennie Nothnagel on the phone half a dozen times, and called the night before to confirm our appointment, but when we got to the address in Second Street, he was out. 'Sometimes they get cold feet,' I said. 'Even though we've been introduced and there's a connection, they suddenly decide it's a scam. They worry they're going to get burgled.'

'You don't look like a criminal,' she said.

'Thank you.'

Hennie's wall would not last: it was leaning out over the pavement as if it might fall the next time the wind blew. Panels between the pillars showed little golfers in silhouette cut from iron sheets. The round heads of the drivers at the top of the backswing created a decorative border like a rolling wave. Beside the gate was the classic golf ball letterbox that had first attracted my attention.

I wrote a note on the back of a business card and dropped it through the slot. 'Please call me.' Probably wouldn't.

Talk talk talk. Making a duck's bill of fingers and thumb. Kwar kwar kwar.

'So, Auerbach,' I said. 'What do you make of him?'

'He's got a bit of a cult following.'

'That bad, hey.'

'I'm not a believer, but . . . but! . . .' She wagged a sinuous exclamation mark out of her forefinger and did something Balinese with her head.

I was reminded of the sign language interpreter who appeared in a window on the TV screen during the news. Life in the digital age. I waited for her to continue, but evidently 'but' was the final word. I asked, 'What photographers do you believe in then?'

'It's not a question of belief. I like to be baffled. Do you know S. Majara? I profiled him last year for the *News* – I'll send you a link – he was so oblique he was facing the other way. Everything he said about his work sounded plausible and yet suspect, as if he'd found it in an article by a shrewdly hostile critic. That's a line from my piece by the way. These days I can't help quoting myself.'

That makes two of us, I thought. 'It must be a technique, going off at a tangent, I mean. It's the attitude I'd like to have, but I wouldn't get away with it. I don't have an interview manner.'

'You have some strategies, you said so yourself.'

'But I haven't had a chance to practise them.'

'You'll just have to be yourself for the time being, Neville. We can't all be S. Majara.'

Even S. Majara isn't S. Majara. His name is Simeon but he had the foresight to give himself a nom de guerre. I can imagine how useful that would be. If only I'd thought of 'N. Lister' before I ever set foot in a gallery.

'Never mind the man, what do you like about his work? I take it the two aren't the same.'

'Slight, light and liminal, quote unquote as if you don't

know. Blink and you'll miss it. "Photograph" is such a heavy word, Majara and I agreed. Even "photo" is dull. You can hear the bell tolling. Phoh!-toh! We should find some other word. Have you noticed how Auerbach always says "photograph" as if he needs to give the thing its full, awful weight. It suits his work too. Those people of his standing around in their gloomy houses like pieces of furniture, holding up their faces like signboards, like beggars at robots. No job, three kids, please help. The whites are the worst, excuse me. I can hardly bear to look at his early stuff. It makes me feel claustrophobic, like I've been locked up in some museum no one visits any more.'

'It was a different time, you know. You're probably too young to remember.'

'Ja, but I don't believe it was all so gloomy.'

'It was horrible! Every day of their lives ordinary people were subjected to appalling abuse. This was a police state, there were soldiers in the townships, activists were being tortured and killed, bombs were going off in burger joints. Business is booming, we used to joke, but it wasn't funny.'

To tell the truth, this was something I'd heard from Leora.

'You had to be there,' Janie said with a laugh.

The phone sneezed again and she glanced at the message distractedly.

'Do you know Majara's *Curious Restitution*?' she asked.

'No.'

'He grinds curios into sawdust and reconstitutes the dust as wooden blocks. There's a whole undercurrent about mincemeat and butcher's blocks and what have you, but it isn't heavy, you know. He makes these abstract assemblages of the blocks, almost like children's toys, that fit together so beautifully you'd think they were made in a lab, like those 3D drawings in resin, and then he takes them apart again and carves them into new curios, which are so much like the originals even the people who made them wouldn't know the difference.'

'But we do.'

'Only because he tells us. He paints them with special pigments derived from the boots of dead miners.'

Surely there was a provocation in this; she was challenging me to contradict her. The boots of dead miners? The boots?

'And how is this photography?'

'Oh, I forgot, he photographs the toys before he carves them up again and makes these tiny black and white prints that look like they came out of a woodworking manual, something a baby boomer got for Christmas, very beautiful in an inconsequential way.'

At the house in Malvern, we had better luck. Antoine K – he insisted on the initial – was waiting for us on the pavement in a sky-blue suit feathered with silver embroidery. The toes of his shoes were as long and pointed as powder horns and tipped with chrome. His presence was not assurance enough for the kids playing soccer in the street and when we pulled up at the kerb they retreated to a wary distance.

The wall behind Antoine was made of old garage doors, five or six of them patched together with sheets from bus shelters and billboards. Best prices, the wall said, fresh petrol. Two breeze-block pillars held a gate of rusty iron panels. Angles of board and corrugated iron stuck out like shark fins above the wall. You would have thought the place was a scrapyard wedged between two houses on a suburban street.

We got out of the car.

'Think I'll take a look around,' Janie said brightly.

'Be careful.'

The backpack clung to her shoulders like a gigantic beetle. Miming some sort of SWAT team procedure, she slipped through the gap in the gate with the digicam cocked. You're not my father.

I greeted Antoine and before our hands unclasped he started talking. He'd given me the outline of his life story on the telephone and now he went on to the unabridged version, starting with the hardships he'd endured in the Congo before escaping to South Africa eight years ago. I let him talk while I set up the camera. It was an epic journey. Although he'd cadged the occasional ride, he seemed to have walked a lot of the way – in more sensible shoes than these, I assumed. The trip had cost him the few items of value he'd left home with, down to the watch off his wrist. When he finally arrived in Johannesburg, he was so poor, he said, he did not even have the time.

My laughter was excessively hearty, I thought. But then so was his. I thought.

On a wooden post beside the gate was a letterbox made of a Wall & All tin with a slot cut in the bottom. Pebble Beach, according to the label, ran in horizontal streaks along the tin, defying gravity. I shooed a few of the bolder children out of the background and asked Antoine to stand next to the letterbox. I wanted him to look at the camera, to look at me, but he kept looking away down the street. I looked too, with the feeling that someone was creeping up on us, although I could see no one there. All the while, he kept talking, showing me the length of his journey, the scale of his suffering, between his outstretched palms.

Before I could take a shot, Janie was back with the denim jacket tied around her waist and a gaggle of kids pointing imaginary cameras, playing follow the leader.

'It's a village back there! You'd never say so, but there must be twenty shacks behind this wall, a whole shanty town in the middle of a suburb. I reckon there could be a hundred people living here. Do you want to take a look?'

'No thanks.'

'You'd get some great shots. It's like the kasbah or something, all these twisty alleyways between the shacks, really beautiful. There's one shack made of ten different materials – iron, hardboard, scraps of lumber, you name it – but the whole thing's been painted eau de Nil. It's an artwork. Have you been to Zanzibar? It's like that, except the scale's all weird because everything's been reduced to fit on one plot. Maybe it's three-quarter scale like Melrose Arch. It has that sort of charm, although it's very different, of course, I don't mean to suggest. When you're done, you should look around.'

'I'd rather not.'

'Why?'

'I don't want the inside story.'

'But aren't you curious?'

'A little.'

'What's the problem then? Don't tell me you're scared.'

'I'm allergic to drama. I can't go poking around in the pitiful contents of strangers' lives. Even the miraculous tales of endurance are too much for me.'

She gave me a look, in conjunction with a hand gesture that was half an insult, and went back through the gap in the gate. I was being indiscreet, I realized, this was another aspect of my interview manner I'd have to brush up on. Rule number one: Never speak your mind. I must remember to tell her it was off the record. A casual 'OTR' will prove I'm in the know.

Antoine was looking at me, almost, with the same disbelieving half-smile and empty-handed gesture, like a father wondering whether he really should embrace the prodigal son. Not that he was old enough to be my father. Down the bells of his colourful sleeves I could see all the way to his skinny chest. Was the suit for special occasions? Or did he wear something this beautiful every day? He was luminous. Fabulous. Fabulosity be damned. Prodigal. Now that's a peculiar word. It means wastefully extravagant, and yet it seems to mean returned home.

I went back to the camera and he went back to telling me about the night last year when a mob armed with knobkieries and golf clubs had driven him out of his shack in Alex. No, not his neighbours, he said, he did not know these people. Except for that one from across the road and his brother. They had brought tyres and petrol and threatened to burn him alive. For the first time since he came to South Africa, he was glad his wife and children were not with him. He was lucky to get away with his life. With the clothes on his back, I thought. As he told how narrowly he had escaped, the space between his hands diminished until they were pressed together in a gesture of prayer.

Much later, when I looked at the photo and Antoine refused to meet my eye, gazing instead down the street, I was reminded of Klee's Angel. He has always been with me, from the door of my room in a Yeo Street commune, to a notice board in Finsbury Park, to the wall of my studio in Leicester Road. I went to look at him again, to see if the resemblance to Antoine was fanciful. There he is, hurtling into the future with his big ears flapping, the furled diplomas of his wingtips raised in surrender, the unravelling scrolls of his hair in a tangle. His face is not turned squarely towards the past. He watches from the corners of his eyes. Even the Angel of History can hardly bear to look.

When we were driving again, she went back to my sense of adventure.

I had to defend myself. 'Every day, I feel more and more like a bloody sociologist. All I'm capable of is making a survey.'

'Whatever happened to the participant observer? You need to explore.'

'I'm past that. Just going out for groceries is a mission.'

'You wouldn't believe how interesting that place is. I might come back and do a proper piece about it. Apparently there are people from all over Africa there, from ten different countries. I'm sure you could see it in the styles of the shacks. This woman told me it's a little version of Addis. Or maybe Luanda.'

A brief, chiming avalanche of currency from the backpack like a fruit machine paying out. She opened the zip and took out the phone, then changed her mind and put it away again without answering.

'Have you heard of urban exploration?'

Another frivolous new discipline, I supposed, like sky polo or extreme proofreading, but it was a serious thing. She had written an article about the urban explorers, men and women on their own voyages of discovery through the backwoods of contemporary life. As wealth and power ebb and flow through an increasingly urbanized world, she said, it's only natural cities should begin to generate their own wildernesses. More and more places that were domesticated – warehouses, power stations, hospitals, hotels, theme parks, film studios – are outliving their uses and becoming derelict. Those that cannot be remodelled fall into disrepair, not going back to nature, exactly, but winding down into wilder, freer states. This is the New World of the urban explorer. Even properties that have been abandoned may be defended, mind you, and entering them takes courage, there is only so much you can learn on Google Earth. Working alone or in teams, the new explorers venture into run-down paradises with cameras and notebooks to enjoy their pleasures and chart their mysteries. I could look on her blog. The codes of conduct are strict: take nothing but photographs, leave nothing but footprints. There are wonderful pictures on the web from Sheffield, Bucharest, Newark and a hundred other places, every bit as exciting as the views of Mars sent back by Viking 1. Images of the future, she said, this is how the world will be when the turbines of development finally seize and things begin to run backwards again.

'I wouldn't last a day,' I told her. 'I have the hiking boots, but I'm not intrepid enough. And I'm not sure we're in the right place for this particular pastime. You'll be taking your life in your hands if you break into a mothballed warehouse in Denver or Cleveland.' I meant the industrial areas of Johannesburg, but the American cities echoed through the names more clearly than usual. 'There are too many trigger-happy security guards running around. You're as liable to be hurt by a militiaman who got his gun licence in a lucky dip – don't quote me – as by some homeless desperado who wants your takkies.'

'The homeless aren't the problem,' she said, 'it's the people with property you need to worry about.'

'I suppose you've met a lot of homeless souls.'

'I have actually. I did a piece on the Homeless World Cup in Cape Town.'

'Always wondered about that. Do they put the players up in hotels or must they take their chances at the city shelter?'

She rolled her eyes.

'No really, it's a heartless question but a fair one. It's about survival, which is your thing. Are the referees homeless too?'

My old friend Sabine called me after her divorce. By then her educational resources agency had grown into a little corporation supplying services to the sector. Human resource development, information technology, knowledge management. I'd done some work for her back in the twentieth century when the deal was IT centres in schools – my moody shots of kids at the keyboard did wonders for the annual report – but we had not seen one another since. Now she was single again and looking for company.

On our first date, we went to Gatrile's in Sandown, her choice, her expense account. While she was sipping her sherry and I was chewing my tongue, Eddie Ledwaba stopped at our table to say hello. The poster boy of BEE, if the business pages can be believed. She remembered him from his trade union days, she told me afterwards, before the Cuban cigars and single malts. He still had a Lenin cap, but he only wore it on public holidays.

Over the mains (rack of lamb for me, sole for the CEO), Sabine told me that she and Bob Heartfield had parted company professionally and personally, in that order. Apparently he'd been caught bending the rules on certain tenders and been allowed to resign to keep his ass out of court. That was the American part of his anatomy she singled out. Soon afterwards, they decided to cut their losses and unbundle the marriage too.

Sabine had a townhouse in Sunninghill and an office in Woodmead. It suited her, this unfinished edge of the city, defined not only by the obvious construction sites, bristling with cranes and scaffolding, but by the leavings of building materials dumped on pavements and empty lots, stacks of bricks, piles of boards and fascias under torn plastic sheets, prefab huts, heaps of rubble and river sand. It was hard to say whether things were half-built or partly demolished. Sex with Sabine had a provisional quality to it too, our bodies never quite fitted together. When I left her place in the early mornings and drove away through the clutter, I had my doubts about the merger.

The headquarters of her company were in an office park near the freeway. The suite was huge and determinedly neutral, with sisal matting on the floor and some sort of ecru canvas on the walls. 'It's all about the finishes,' Sabine said to me when she gave me the guided tour. Besides the MD, no one had an office as such; people sat at workstations in odd corners, perched on the edges of their ergonomically designed chairs as if they had just paused for a moment to skim through a spreadsheet or rattle off an email. Sabine's office was so huge it made her enormous desk look small. The only other items in the room were a chair for visitors, in which I sat like a truant, and a chocolate-brown ceramic pot containing a tree covered with waxy leaves and tiny oranges. African contemporary, she said, under contract. In winter, the pot was replaced by an ivory urn and three long wands of pampas grass. The air conditioner hummed to itself. One blade in the wooden blind droned along sympathetically.

You would think that things were winding down here, being wound up. They must be on the point of moving: soon they would carry out the last few filing cabinets and switch off the lights. But the impression was mistaken. Sabine assured me that they were not going anywhere, they had been in their new premises for a year and they were settling in very nicely. The building was brilliant. You couldn't ask for better finishes at the price.

The atmosphere of places made to be abandoned clung like cigarette smoke in my clothes. You were not meant to grow attached to them, and it was scarcely possible because they offered no purchase. The almost-unpacked, never-lived-in look was the mark of success. Everyone was a fly-by-nighter.

Our love affair was not entirely unpleasant. My side of it was pure curiosity and for her it was a case of getting back into the market with a low-risk investment. We had a lot of fun. I thought she overdid the throaty laughter under the duvet, but before I could take offence, we went back to being friends, and then not.

We turned off the N3 and drove back towards Sunninghill. I had not been in the area for years and it still seemed incomplete. Janie held her camera out of the window and took photos. My friends in the trade insist that photos are made rather than taken, but she was a taker. She took samples, clipping them out of the fabric of the unspooling world at arm's length and barely glancing at the screen to see what was there.

On Witkoppen Road, I pulled over, turned the volume down on Classic FM, which I'd been using to staunch the flow of talk, and opened the Map Studio. Sunninghill Extension 11, where Aurelia Mashilo lived, was not in the book yet.

'You need a Garmin,' Janie said.

'God no, I don't want to go around like a pigeon with a ring on my leg. I'll leave that to your intrepid explorers.'

'But if you had GPS, you would never get lost.'

'I know.'

I did have a new map of Gauteng, which I'd fetched from the AA in Park Meadows the day before. We unfolded it on the dash and found Sunninghill Extensions 9 and 10. With a bit of luck Extension 11 would be where it seemed to fit, like a puzzle piece, in one of the few patches of pale-green veld left on the edge of the suburb.

There's an art to folding the flat earth into a pocketbook: you must learn to read the curvature of a crease, the lie of the paper land. I should write a guide to the subject, I thought as I refolded the map, and she can put it on her blog with the survival tips.

'Why don't you call and get directions,' she said.

'Let's first see if we can find it.'

It was townhouse territory, complex country. One walled city after another, separated by remnants of open veld. Some of the vacant plots were covered with tall grass; others had been burnt to blackened stubs, revealing huge molehills of rubble. A few men waiting on a corner for work barely glanced at the Charade, supposing that no building contractor would drive such a thing. As if to demonstrate their own ingenuity as builders, they had fashioned seats from the rubble, miniature stonehenges of bricks or stools of half-bricks and planks, which allowed them to swivel managerially without raising their elbows from their knees. Casual labour.

'I've got software on my phone that lets me keep track of my friends,' she said.

'Why would you want to do that?'

'For laughs, mainly, but it's also a security. I mean, if someone gets hijacked or whatever, you can find out where they are. I wouldn't like to get a puncture out here.'

Extension 11 was a small, exclusive addition to the suburb, two blocks of newly built mansions behind towering walls. We negotiated the boom and cruised between the sun-struck cliffs, looking for the number. Here and there, through gaps in the defences, we caught sight of grey modernist bunkers, late Tuscan villas, contemporary African homesteads with walls in shades of mud and ochre.

Leora's sister Jacqui, who is a landscape gardener, had found Aurelia Mashilo's place for me. The photo she'd emailed had not done it justice. The wall was a cubist assemblage of nut-brown plaster, corrugated-iron parallelograms and pale drystone panels, somewhere on the trade route between Mali and Malibu. The gate was made of stainless-steel quatrefoils. A swathe of broken stone, like a half-built Roman road, lay in the shadow of the wall in place of a garden. On either side of the gate was an alcove lined with pigeon-blue slate and grilled with iron bars. These niches seemed custom-made for a Venus de Milo from Makro or a David from the Builders Warehouse, but they were empty.

As if to make up for this lack, the letterbox, which was of particular interest to me, was in the form of a nymph holding a slotted cornucopia under her arm. Ceres, I thought, or Proserpine (now and then I am grateful for my beginner's year of Classics).

Aurelia buzzed us in, the shiny gate opened and I drove up on to a blood-red piazza. On that vast expanse of Coro-brik, the Daihatsu felt smaller than a Cinquecento. The house behind the wall was an equally intriguing blend of pillars, pediments, stainless steel and layered stone. Aurelia was in the portico defying the elements in an earth-toned frock and silver sandals.

'Sun Goddess,' Janie said. 'How did she make her money again? I'll bet her husband gave it to her.'

'She earned a pile of it herself. Not that he's on the bones of his backside. She used to be in fashion, but now she devotes her time to charity and sits on a board or two.'

'And how did he get rich?'

'The South African way. Mining.'

Actually, I had a soft spot for David Mashilo, the former Robben Islander known for his business savvy and his sports cars. I had also spent ten years against my will on a small, inhospitable island, although to my discredit I had not used the opportunity to get a BCom.

I wasn't sure where to put the car. In the end, I just switched off the engine where we were and we walked over to the house. Aurelia was more beautiful than her photographs, and taller too, what with the hair extensions piled on her shapely head. Under her arm she had a small hairy dog, which she shifted over to the other hip to shake my hand. She was vivacious and charming. She wanted us to come in for tea and cake, and the cool marble entrance hall was inviting, but I said we were running late. 'We'll lose the light.' How often have I said that? Even at noon, it happens. She was going to insist, I think, but changed her mind when she saw the digicam.

I got my camera bags and we walked down to the street.

Aurelia and the mail nymph. It was perfect. She wanted to leave the gate open, so that the house would be visible in the background; my explanations about the wall and the street, my half-truths about the public and the private, already presented in a string of emails and repeated now, made no sense to her. The sun blared from the stainless-steel panels and my eyes began to burn. When I was on the point of giving up, it occurred to me to mention that if the gate stayed open the Charade would be in the picture too, and then she relented. But once the gate had closed, she became anxious out in the street – on foot, as she put it. A security guard with a nightstick had wandered closer from a hut at the end of the block, but if anything he seemed to make her more nervous. The dog began to yap. She buzzed the house and spoke through the intercom. In a while a young man in a nacreous suit and pimpish winkle-pickers that Antoine would have died for, wearing a holstered pistol on his belt, came to stand guard while we worked. The security cameras perched like crows on the wall dropped their beaked faces to watch. She was making big eyes and sucking in her cheeks, some crazy technique for looking good on film. The woman had been a fashion model. I wondered how I could make her stop and still get a decent shot. Meanwhile, in my shady interior, which smells of old ice and bloody polystyrene, Mr Frosty was whispering, 'Drop the dog, drop the dog.'

'Tell me about the survival tips.' We were driving back to Kensington.

'Some of it's survival per se, with a capital S, and some of it's health and leisure. Search on Wellness.'

'For instance?'

She bit her knuckle. 'Okay. Stuff about cars. Not just the obvious like leaving your windows open a crack so they're harder to break in a smash-and-grab, everybody knows that by now, including the guys with the spark plugs. More conceptual things. Say you lose your car at Makro or Gold Reef City or whatever. If you press the remote the car will squeal and let you know where it is. It's like whistling for a dog. A friend of mine found his car like this in a blizzard once. He saw the lights flashing under a metre of snow.'

'That's pretty impressive.'

'It was in Sweden. Every society has its problems, even if it looks perfect from the outside.'

'What else?'

'Couple of tips from Oprah. Let's say someone locks you in the boot of a car, what do you do? You kick out a tail light, put your arm through the hole and wave. Hopefully there's someone following who understands that this is a crisis. Sometimes you have to be your own hero, quote unquote.'

'It sounds heavy.'

'We're living in dangerous times so, ja, it's a bit rough. But a lot of it is really useful too. I try to soften the impact by putting in some uplifting sidebars. For instance, true-life stories of survival against the odds. Have you heard of Little Milo Babić?'

'No.'

'He's the poster child of survival. During the siege of Sarajevo, his mom made him a survival kit in case something happened to her or they were separated. She knitted him a jersey with his name and address in the pattern, and he had a backpack with sandwiches and juice, a change of clothes and a space blanket, his favourite storybook and a miniature album of family photos. His picture got into the papers and he became known all over the world.'

'Did he survive?'

'Sure, he's not so little any more, he's all grown up and working as a butcher in Emmarentia. I want to do a piece on him some time. I've made contact.'

'He must be full of tips.'

'You know what's the best survival tip I've come across?'

'No.'

'Okay, listen up, this might save your life. Don't touch your eyes when you're at the mall. I'm serious. That's the best way to pick up an infection in a public place: take some bug off the escalator rail or the supermarket trolley handle on the tip of your finger and put it into your body via your eyeball. Smart move. The eye is the window of the immune system. What you need to do is keep your hands at your sides or in your pockets and as soon as you get home, give them a good wash. Never mind if your eyes start itching in the Pick n Pay, you can learn not to scratch.'

Vienna Butchery makes the best schnitzel rolls in town, but you need a strong stomach for the decor. A jungle of pot plants on the counters and herds of hunting trophies on the walls have turned the place into a garish diorama. Looking down from on high, their eyes unnaturally bright, their ears permanently pricked for the rustle of predators among the ferns and rubber plants, the heads of the antelopes make the blood run in the fridges. Suddenly the meat looks freshly slaughtered. As soon as our order had been placed, Janie went to wait outside, and she was quiet as we drove back to Leicester Road.

Grabbing two plates off the rack in the kitchen, I led her out to my studio, where there is an excess of plain sunlight. The workspace has windows from floor to ceiling, and on top of that skylights it does not really need, a double-volume shed filled with light to balance the dense cube of the darkroom. I sat in the wicker chair at the door, with my legs stretched out to catch the sun, and she browsed as she ate, glancing over the contents of my pinboard, occasionally lifting the corner of a cutting with her little finger to see what was underneath.

'What's all this?' she asked.

'Bits and pieces.'

'Reference material? Research?'

'That sort of thing, yes.'

'This looks like it came out of a Christmas cracker.'

'It's quite possible.'

The yellow card with the deaf alphabet on one side and a request for a donation on the other had been handed to me by a young man at the airport on my last trip. She hinged the card aside on its pin, chewed and swallowed, and read from the strip of paper beneath: 'What does history know of nail-biting?' Her eyebrows arched into a question.

'Arthur Koestler.'

'Cool.'

How can I say what these fragments mean to me? The awkward truths of my life take shape in their negative spaces. In the lengthening shadows of the official histories, looming like triumphal arches over every small, messy life, these scraps saved from the onrush of the ordinary are the last signs I can bring myself to consult.

Thank God for the sandwich. Had her hands been free, she'd have used the camera to take a note or two. Just for reference.

The Black Magic box stood empty on the end of a trestle table. She raised the lid by its tassel and studied the drawings of nut clusters and liqueur creams on the underside.

'World capital of nougat,' she said.

'What?'

'Montélimar. In the south of France.'

'Oh.'

'Is this cool or what? It's like Forrest Gump except all the chocolates have been scoffed.'

The dead letters were laid out on a card table covered in green baize. Initially, I'd arranged them by the size and colour of the envelopes, later by postal code, and finally as they are now by handwriting, an entirely subjective order based on perceived affinities between the slope of an l and a t or the morse of dotted i's.

'And this?'

'My next project.'

I am turning into a person with projects. I've always hated that word. I wiped my fingers and went over to the table.

'What are they?' she asked.

'Dead letters.'

'That will scare away the punters. What does it mean?'

'Letters that didn't reach their destination. They were posted, but for one reason or another they were never delivered.'

'Are they real?'

'Oh yes.'

'Where did you get them?'

'They were left to me. It's a long story.'

'Try me, I'm not in a hurry.'

'I can't.'

'So they're found objects.'

'Lost objects.'

'Not stolen?'

'Lost.'

'I've heard of letters being dumped in the veld by a lazy postman. If that's the story here, you should turn them over to the authorities.'

'That's not it. They were given to me, as I said, a long time ago. Anyway, it's never been clear who the authorities are in this case.'

'And the people who posted them, do they know where their letters are now?'

I shook my head.

Without a by-your-leave, as my mother would say, she held one of the envelopes up to the window. Against the light, the dark blade of a folded page floated askew in its filmy container. For a moment she was lost in thought.

'Have you opened any of them?'

'No, although I've been tempted.'

'I'm sure I couldn't resist.'

'It's private correspondence, long delayed, but still.'

'I take it you're going to use them in your next project.'

'Yes.'

'Is that okay?' she insisted. 'I mean, they don't belong to you.'

'I told you already they were given to me.'

'Do you have the right to keep them though?'

'As much as the next person.'

'What are you going to do with them?'

'I'm not sure yet, that's the problem. Maybe I'll deliver them.'

'Some of the addresses are barely legible.' She leaned closer to the display. 'What does this say? I can't make it out.'

'I still have to decipher it myself.'

'These are really old too. Where have they been all this time? Did they fall down the back of some filing cabinet? Is that it? You can tell me.'

'No, I can't, and I don't want you writing about it either.'

'Look at the stamps. C.R. Swart. He was the President, right? People will have moved. You'll never be able to deliver them.'

'Maybe I'll just work out the addresses and go and drop them in the boxes. I won't even ring the doorbell.'

'That's pretty hopeless, Neville. There has to be a better solution than that.'

'I could take a picture of the letterbox.'

'No ways, not good enough.'

'Why not? Let whoever gets the letter make of it what they will. Isn't that always the case?'

'There's an art to expressing your failures fully, if you don't mind me saying so. You need to find the people these letters were intended for, it's the only way open to you, ethically and aesthetically.'

'Sounds like work for a private eye.'

'Find the people and talk to them,' she said. 'Can you imagine the stories!'

'I'm not a storyteller. I wish I was interested in stories, other people's especially, but I'm not.'

'You never know the lives people have lived until you ask, and asking is an obligation.' Lecturing me now. 'Every time someone dies, a whole history dies with them. It's like each one of us is an archive.'

'I'm surprised you're so interested in the past.'

'Oh, I'm all for it, so long as there aren't too many grumpy people involved. I'm not exactly a born-free, but I'm not a child of apartheid either. I don't need all that misery.'

'People suffered terribly under apartheid, you know.'

'Ja, but it's time to move on.'

When I was a child, it puzzled me that there were so many films about the War, that the model planes were Spitfires and Stukas, and the comics were full of Germans shouting, 'Achtung!' Why was this ancient conflict so alive? My grandpa had been up north, but he was ancient too and belonged in another era. As I got older it became obvious. Scarcely twenty years had passed since the atom bombs were dropped on Japan. The earth was still trembling. I can feel it trembling now.

We had our own brief lifespans to consider. Janie asked for a copy of my CV and I went inside to print one in Leora's study. 'You can email it,' she called after me, but I wanted to get it done.

When I came back, she was watching her footage on the digicam.

'Check this out!'

I went with her into the maze of Antoine's village, twisting and turning between the shacks, on and on as if the place were endless. Once she came to a dead end, quickly doubled back, and found another path. The shacks were so close together, you could reach out and touch the walls on either side. A tangible community. You would not need to go next door for a cup of sugar, you could simply lean out of your window. She swung around a corner, jaunty and unafraid. A woman stooping over a plastic basin of laundry started when she saw her, and then stood up with her foamy hands on her hips, laughing. She focused on the laughing woman and then on a king-size bottle of Sta-soft. 'Hello ma. Who are you? Tell me your name and what you're doing.' But the camera made the woman shy and she turned away, hiding her face. The camera bobbed and reeled again along the ironclad streets, as if it had been set adrift on a raft. Bits of sky flickered into the lens, dented walls fell like shutters, layers of trampled earth flew up. She turned to look back. A gang of kids were following her, excited and alarmed. She focused on a girl with braids standing out stiffly like a crown of exclamation marks all around her head.

I offered to drive her home, but she had called a cab already and it was waiting when I let her out.

On the threshold, she paused and said, 'One last thing: I need you with your letterbox, obviously.'

'It's just a slot in the wall.'

She held the camera out and looked at the screen. The way I study packages in the supermarket when I forget my reading glasses, trying to see how much salt they contain. She said, 'I see what you mean. Two peas in a pod. Okay, say something cheesy.'

'And in the alcoves?'

'Nothing.'

'You sure?' Leora inspected the print as if there might be some small object in the shadows. 'They must be displaying something.'

'No, nothing.'

'Weird. What is this style, African Imperial? Sol Kerzner must be behind it, he was the great prophet of the African Renaissance.'

'I think it's what Aurelia calls Afrocentric chic.'

I put the prints on the dresser and began to set the table while Leora went back to chopping fennel on the butcher's block. It was Friday evening. The aromatic essence of her famous salmon soufflé – in individual ramekins, if you don't mind – came from the eye-level oven; a salad cut down cruelly in its youth, baby carrots, bean sprouts, young spinach leaves, lay in a bamboo bowl. While she mixed the dressing, I opened some wine (it was a compensatory Springfield Life from Stone, nursed to maturity in the rocky soils of the Robertson valley) and told her more about the day with Janie.

'Tell me, Mr Lister, was it a good interview?'

Leora's sense of humour: Mr Lister of Leicester Road. 'It was more like a natter with a friend. She didn't shut up for a second. Talk talk talk.'

'What about?'

'Let's see. Saul Auerbach, the godfather of documentary photography. Metaphysical acupuncture, the new thing. How to get chewing gum out of a budgie. Her dreams and ambitions.'

'I thought she was interviewing you.'

'I made the mistake of asking.'

'Never show an interest. That's the first law of self-promotion.'

'I wish I'd known.'

'What are her ambitions then?'

'She wants to be a brand ambassador.'

'For what?'

'Herself, I think. She wants her own talk show and to grow and grow and be the best Janie she can be. She could give inspirational talks to young people on overcoming adversity, it's just that nothing really shit has happened to her yet.'

I was being unfair, but I couldn't stop.

Leora is a nicer person than I am, but she secretly admires and sometimes encourages this side of me. 'She might have to settle for something in the performing arts,' she said, pumping the juice out of a lemon as if she were doing reps at the gym, 'poetry, say, or weather forecasting . . .'

'The trick is to diversify. She's writing a cookery book and a children's book and a children's cookery book. There's a CD in the pipeline: some minor mogul overheard her scatting in the fitting rooms at the Zone and signed her to his label. Meanwhile, she's working on a screenplay set in the future when we've run out of gas and everyone's living in ruined Tuscan villages and puttering around in solar-powered golf carts.'

'She sounds like a live wire.'

'She'll be an oober-something-or-other.'

'You're quite taken with her.'

'It was like talking to a time traveller, a mime artist from a distant galaxy come to assure us that all will be well.'

Enough. Leora peeped into the oven, liberating a soothing waft of nutmeg.

'And how did your side of the conversation go?'

'Not well. I cast around for a story, some credible version of myself to impart, but I couldn't find one. This pop stuff is infectious. I started coughing up factoids like a column in the newspaper. Not a columnist, note, a column, one of those last-ditch efforts to look like a website.'

'You couldn't find a story?'

'No, I've dropped the thread and I can't be bothered to pick it up again. I'm all thumbs anyway. What holds my attention now is design. Show me a pattern in the information and I'm satisfied.'

Leora tasted the salad dressing on the tip of her finger.
'She was being ironic, obviously,' she said.
'Yes.'
'And so are you.'
'I guess.'
'The whole thing is ironic.'
'Including the ironies.'
'Maybe they cancel one another out then,' Leora said,
'like a double negative.'

She put on the oven gloves that look like sharks and
brought the bowls to the table in their soft jaws, the *individual ramekins*, each with a little chef's hat of gilded egg.
'Poor baby,' carving out a spoonful of soufflé and raising
it to my mouth, 'here.'

Channel-hopping with the sound down is my kind of
extreme sport: there is always a story to be gaffed from
the sea of televised images. The tide is rising there too, it's
another case of global warming. Every day, an immense
shelf of information drifts out into the channels, data, use-
less entertainment, dogma, edifying documentaries, reality shows, weather reports, travel advice, sport, opinions,
views, news, views, news. Mainly, because I have been in
a gloomy mood, news of the dead and dying. Two hundred
feared drowned as ferry capsizes. Suicide bomber kills thirty
in Baghdad market. Twelve die as bus plunges off bridge.

Teenager slays mother, brother, self. Nearly 140 cases of horse sickness reported in KwaZulu-Natal. The fatalities keep ticking while the news hounds find another tree to bark up. All the correspondents appear to be embedded somewhere. Even the girl reporting on the interprovincial netball in Potch is tinged with the war-zone green. We are so used to human bombs scattering fragments of their own flesh like leaflets in the rubble that we hardly notice the numbers killed.

Unwilling to watch any of it through to the end, I do my research (Mr Lister's Festival of Films with Peculiar Accents, coming soon to a multiplex near you); and when I weary of that, I piece together my own staccato sub-plots, ranging across the channels, leaping from one floe to another, taking as material whatever wildlife documentary or cookery show or courtroom drama or soap opera I land in. One jab of the remote and a round fired in Hollywood brings down an antelope in Mala Mala. A serial killer is always on the loose somewhere, and if he's wielding a knife I can get him to chop onions, and use those pungent shards to make the survivors of the latest mudslide weep. Cooking, shooting, weeping, these three abide, 24/7.

The remarkable thing is how it all cuts. There is so much afloat, it's impossible to create a clash, let alone a contradiction, and my improvisations can scarcely be told apart from the scheduled programmes. Chaos is a kind of congruence. Everything has jumped out of its skin, everything is raw and ready to be remixed. In the deluge of contiguity, things that are self-contained, that persist on their own course and refuse new relationships, cannot be endured.

These were the late, late hours of our Friday evening, the end of our end-of-the-working-week routine. Leora and I had eaten supper, finished a bottle of wine, watched a DVD. Her choice one week, mine the next. Last Friday, mine: *Dances with Wolves*. I had been calling her Stands with a Spoon all week and it was time to move on. Tonight, hers: *Pride and Prejudice*. No obvious jokes there. Now she was asleep beside me on the couch with the top of her cherished head pressing against my thigh, and I was flossing my teeth, savouring the exotic combination of minted wax and twelve-year-old scotch. In the uncharted reaches of the menu, between a documentary on Roman ossuaries and reruns of classic frames from the world snooker champs in Leicester, I found him: Jaco Els.

Chef Giacomo of the Paragon Laboratory. Still sleek, almost dapper. Thicker around the middle, but the chef's tunic flattered. It was a vaguely military tunic with silver buttons and epaulettes, and the toque was not the usual tall mushroom but an oversized beret. Giacomo! It's all Italy now. Whatever became of Greece?

Back in the '90s, when the TRC hearings were on television, I'd watched as much as I could stand, hoping to plug the gaps in my knowledge and reanimate the deadened nerve-endings of my sympathy. Among the perpetrators, a long line of men whose memories were as badly made as their suits, I'd always expected to see someone I knew, someone like Jaco. And here he was, ten years too late, giving truthful testimony on the Paragon range of non-stick cookware.

Chef Giacomo was in command of a postmodern kitchen, the kind made for deconstructive cooking. Hi-tech finishes concealed traditional carcases. There was a coal stove with a stainless-steel hob, there were worm-eaten cabinets with granite tops, copper pots hung from steel-plated ceiling beams. Behind pale-green frosted glass that made the cabinets look like shower cubicles were the hazy feminine forms of glasses and bowls. Hollowware, they call it in the trade. On the end of the counter stood a Bunsen burner.

Leora would have loved it and I thought of waking her up. But the sight of Jaco after all these years was too strange: I needed to absorb it on my own.

I thumbed up the volume.

Maestro! Time had knocked the rough edges off his accent and there was a twang in there now that intrigued: he sounded like a spray painter from Roodepoort who's been to Bible School in San Antonio. It made his storytelling more compelling than ever. In a minute, I was drawn in. While he described the unique properties of the Paragon's non-stick coating, he settled a pan on a gas ring and turned up the heat. He showed us a bottle of sunflower oil and tossed it in the bin. He showed us a brick of butter and sent that south too.

Sticky stuff was lined up in tubs beside the stove, and he reached for them and dribbled honey and jam into the pan, and spooned in sugar and custard powder. He made it bubble, added a handful of flour and gave it a good stir with a spatula. Then he poured the goo out and broke an egg into the empty pan.

Where exactly is a twang, I wonder. I would like a linguist to explain it to me. And why San Antone? Why not Tulsa or Forth Worth?

While the egg was frying, he showed us a pot scourer and tossed it in the bin. He spoke about the damage caused by steel wool and abrasive scouring agents, ickcetera. He tossed aside brushes, pads and soap-impregnated pillows.

When the egg was done, he slid it on to a plate, put the empty pan back on the gas and turned up the heat until the flame formed a blue calyx around the black iron base. He spoke about the special guarantee, but that's not all, he mentioned special prices if you dialled now. He said that if something stuck to a Paragon, they would give you your money back. While he was speaking, he took from under the counter a thick, rainbow-striped beach sandal and dropped it in the pan. Easing a paper mask over his mouth and nose, he fired up a blowtorch and played it over the rubber until it smoked and bubbled and began to melt. Prices and order numbers flashed in jagged clouds. Jaco reached for the spatula again and pressed the molten sole down in the pan. The smell of burning rubber filled the room.

My knees are packing up, my mother would say, and my back's already gone out. Quoting Shelley Winters, I think. Now this business with her eyes. She'd woken up with double vision. Hoping it would go away, as the aches and pains usually did, she'd held out for a week before making an appointment with Dr Jacobson, who did her cataracts. 'You should see me trying to decide which of my faces to powder,' she said when she phoned, making light, working her way round to asking for a lift to the clinic. We've spoken about moving her into a retirement village or a home, some place with frail care for when the time comes, you have to think ahead, but she loves the flat. She has friends in the block, widows like herself, decent bridge players. And she values her independence. Not being able to drive is the worst.

Herbert got up from his desk in the lobby to usher us out of the lift and then took her other arm with the decorous familiarity of a son-in-law. He even held the door of the Charade while I helped her into the passenger seat. I always worry she'll bang her head, more so since her eyes started troubling her, and I was glad of the help. How much was it worth though? Recently Leora had rebuked

me for giving a car guard two rand. Apparently the standard rate had risen to five. I gave that to Herbert and he
seemed satisfied.

'We should have kept the Merc,' my mother said as we
drove off. 'You and Herbert could have carried me down
on a stretcher and stashed me in the back seat.'

'You always were a back-seat driver.'

Letting that pass, she asked: 'How's the work going?'

In my mother's vocabulary, 'work' means what you do
for a living. I told her about the shoot that morning. We'd
been on Constitution Hill, in one of the cold, narrow cells
at the old Women's Jail, dropping crockery on the concrete
floor, clay pots and china cups called Annemarie, Busi,
Caroline, and so on down the alphabet. A public service ad
on spousal abuse. By the time we were finished, the place
looked like a Greek restaurant.

We moved on to other things. I thought of telling her
about the interview for the *News*, but my nascent career
as an 'artist' still embarrasses me in front of the family. I
am much too old to bud. Giacomo Els and his shtick – his
non-shtick – might amuse her. Or it might remind her of
my father, which is not always a good thing. She still has
her wit and her wits about her, but these days she'll get
sad in the blink of an eye. To play it safe, I told her about
the catering business Leora is setting up with her friend
Bo. Before they've even registered the company, they're
arguing about the colour of the table linen.

My mother was reminded of the shenanigans at body corporate meetings, which she attends purely for the theatre. Now the members were at war over the redecoration. 'That old queen Paul Meagher wants lilac tiles in the lobby!' she said. 'It will look like a bathhouse, which is where he got the idea, I think.'

In the parking lot at the Garden City, as I was about to get out of the car, she put her hand on my arm and said, 'Is everything all right?'

'I've been out of sorts,' I said. 'This place gets to me sometimes.'

'What is it now?'

'Nothing specific, a succession of small irritations with the way things work, or don't work, as the case may be.'

'Tell me, before we go in.'

'Here's an example. I was at Home Affairs in Randburg last week to renew my passport. I hadn't been out that way for ages. First I couldn't find the place because I was looking for Hans Strijdom and the name has changed. I've heard Malibongwe Drive on the traffic report a hundred times and I didn't put it together. Then there was a queue a mile long. You'd think it was an election. When I finally got to the counter, they wanted a copy of my old passport, but they didn't have a photocopier, it was broken. The clerk sent me into the parking lot and there was a guy out there with a photocopier rigged to a 12 volt battery. He made me a copy for five rand.

'The whole transaction was so half-baked, so under-developed. And there was a backscratching tone to it, the photocopy guy must be a cousin of the guy behind the counter, he probably takes a cut. They have a little business going on the side, they're in the photocopy racket. The machine in the office, the proper machine, probably isn't even broken. And if it is, why don't they bloody well get it fixed?

'The photocopy guy was eating a chicken breast. He wiped his fingers carefully on a rag, took my passport and hunkered down between two cars. The device was in a tatty cardboard box held together with packaging tape, and he flipped open the lid and got the copy going. My glum, official face edged out of the slot into the sunshine, burnt out, overexposed. This process shouldn't be happening outdoors, I thought, it belongs in a quiet, dust-free, well-lit office. I looked across the street and there behind a palisade fence was some hi-tech head office where people behind cool grey glass were working at terminals in air-conditioned quiet. That's where I should be doing this, I thought again, in a carpeted open-plan office with a water cooler, in an American space, not on a dusty, potholed patch of tar with the sun burning the back of my neck and the smell of fried chicken in the air.

'I paid the guy and went inside with my photocopy. I'd been on the point of complaining about the quality of the print, which made me look like a ghost, but when I got it out of the sunlight it wasn't too bad.'

'So it all worked out in the end.'

'Well, that's what Leora said. When I told her the story, how the whole thing made me feel depressed and anxious about the future, she said it all depends on your perspective. It sounded quite hopeful to her, quite efficient and convenient. My photocopy guy is the African entrepreneur in action. He's found a niche, he's providing an ingenious solution to a problem and making an honest living. It's a sign that things are working. They're just working in a different way.

'And I said, sure, I see that things *can* work this way – but I don't think they *should*.'

'You'll have to get used to it, Nev.'

'Or not. For the first time in years, I've been thinking I might be better off in England, somewhere the world meets my expectations more closely. But I'm not even sure about that. Everything seems harder to manage these days, and stranger. Perhaps it's part of getting old.'

'Wait till you're my age,' she said. 'I can hardly follow what people are saying any more. My ears are nearly as bad as my eyes. I was watching telly the other night and I thought I'd flipped over to the wrong channel. It looked like a quiz show from Bulgaria or something. And then I recognized that chappie from *Strictly Come Dancing* and I realized they were speaking English.'

I'm growing into my father's language: it will fit me eventually like his old overcoat that was once two sizes too big.

We went inside. An aide came with a wheelchair, but she wanted to walk. 'Arrive in one of those and God knows what you'll leave in.' The lobby had a low, subtly shadowed ceiling, bloated sofas in private corners and paintings steeped in lukewarm pools of light. The wrought-iron tables and chairs belonged to the coffee shop. It felt more like a hotel than a clinic. We made for the lifts in baby steps. I realized again how much she's shrunk over the years, she barely reaches my shoulder. Clinging to my arm, and blinking in wonder as she looked around, she seemed like a delicate child being taken on an outing to cheer her up.

Dr Jacobson had his own waiting room. There were pot plants with enormous leaves, which proved to be real, and posters showing the human eye in cross section. It brought back bits and pieces of my long-forgotten school Biology, the rods and cones, the blind spot, the aqueous humour.

I looked at the man on the cover of *Longevity*. His age was a mystery to me.

'Do you ever do popcorn?' my mother asked earnestly. 'In the microwave?'

The nurse behind the counter tensed.

'No . . .'

'Good, because it's making people sick. Popcorn lung.'

'Popcorn lung!'

'You get it from exposure to microwaved popcorn, the artificial butter flavour, to be precise. It's a completely new affliction.'

'Talk about death, disability and dread disease! The insurers must be reeling.'

'You can laugh, but it's the scourge of our times, every bit as horrible as consumption.'

Janie emailed to say she'd posted her first impressions on her blog. As soon as the article was done, she'd let me know. She'd looked again at my thresholders – they were more like gatekeepers, to be frank, just a thought – and for all the lack of drama in the pictures, found them engaging. They had a cumulative effect.

Had I heard of gate trauma? A dozen South Africans are killed by electronic gates every year. Closing gates cause a third of the fatalities, while falling gates account for the rest.

Some thoughts about the dead letters, btw: 'You're making them up. Heard it on the grapevine. So the ethical question – Whose letters? – yields to an aesthetic one – How convincing are they? Well done on clearing that hurdle. I picture you bent over your bench like a monk, with a stack of antique stationery under your fist and an old air-mail sticker on the tip of your tongue, stuff you've been hoarding for ever and at last have a use for. Pretending to be someone you're not, inventing signatures for your alter egos, making up weird handwritings and breaking English into little pieces.'

The digital grapevine: now there's a poisoned plant. I wrote back: 'Would hate to be accused of authenticity, but don't believe everything you hear in the whispering galleries of the internet. No one knows about the dead letters except you and Leora, whose lips are sealed.' It didn't seem appropriate to mention my mother.

The first impressions were cut to a pop song, perhaps one of her own. The tune burbled along like a cellphone ringing underwater. Small animated shrieks zipped out and faded like rockets, while larger groans thumped in the bottom of the pot like root vegetables. Antoine K's shanty town and Aurelia Mashilo's palazzo. Street corners, flyovers rushing closer, bursting into the slipstream like surf, letterboxes, shrubbery, an ejaculation of soapsuds across a dirty windscreen, a braid coiled on the pavement like a house snake, capering children, here and there against a scudding backdrop my solemn profile, my double chin, my hands on the steering wheel, steering. The designated driver. Neville the Navigator.

I went to see Saul Auerbach. This was a few years after the walkabout at the Pollak, where I'd failed to introduce myself; and a few years before my late start at the Switch Box, where I showed my photos of walls. I took some of those prints with me, the first I ever made, thinking I might ask Auerbach to look at them, let him cast a beady eye or a blessing. But when I drew up outside the house in Craighall Park, it seemed presumptuous and I left the pictures in the car.

Still at the same address after all these years. People take root in places, it gets to the point where they cannot imagine being anywhere else and it's too much trouble to move.

Auerbach came to the gate in his trademark khaki shorts (as the papers would put it) and a worn pair of combat boots. He was smaller, bonier and browner than I remembered.

Another visitor was just leaving, a tall man of about sixty wearing a fawn linen suit, impeccably crumpled, and a doffable panama with rising damp on the crown. We shook hands on the pavement – Matti Someone-or-other, a photojournalist from Finland – and then he got into an Audi with Budget stickers in the windows and drove away. An intrepid explorer with an expense account and a hotel room in Sandton. You could imagine that he had just got off a paddle steamer, but not that he would die soon of a fever.

As Auerbach ground beans for the espresso machine, the aromatic details of my last visit to his house swirled into my head. The place had not changed much in twenty years, but whereas I had felt then that I was stepping back in time, now I seemed to be lurching forward. I glanced into the lounge to see if the Swedish chrome and Afghan kilims were still there. That archaic term 'futuristic' came

into my head. It was not that fashion had caught up with
the house, but that the house had gone on ahead. Quotation
was a curse. It was no longer possible to imagine a different future, let alone a better one. Tomorrow always looked
like a recycled version of yesterday. It was already familiar.

When we were seated in the garden at opposite ends
of a long wrought-iron table, the espresso cups steaming
before us, mine host in the full glare of the sun, toasting
himself lightly, yours truly in the shade of a frangipani, I
reminded him about that day.

'Your father was worried you were smoking pot,' he
said, 'and I soon began to think it might be worse, although
I had no idea what I was meant to do about it. You were so
silent and morose for a young man.'

A strange impression I must have made, a boy dressed
like a professor, chewing on a pipe with a plumber's bend
and fouling the air with my ditch-digger's tobacco, brooding.

'His real concern was that I would end up sweeping
the streets, which then marked the bottom of the scale,' I
said. 'He looked to you to set me on a brighter career path.'

'Obviously worked,' Auerbach said with a grim laugh.
When I called to arrange the visit, I'd mentioned that I
was a photographer.

There was not much left of the day in Auerbach's
memory. What for me had been a revelation, had for him
been another working shift, only slightly out of the routine. He remembered Veronica and Mrs Ditton, of course,

232

he remembered the photographs; and that it was poor old Gerald Brookes, whose ticker packed up in a hotel room somewhere back in the '90s, who'd started the game with the houses up on Langermann Kop. But he'd forgotten that I was also there. 'Look, it was a long time ago,' he said, 'but was that really all the same day?'

'Yes, I picked a house too, the house next door to Mrs Ditton's. You were supposed to take a third photo, but we never got round to it.'

'Let me guess: we lost the light.'

'The light waned, yes, and also the interest, I think. Years later, I went back to satisfy my curiosity. I knocked on the door, if you don't mind, and the lady of the house let me in.'

'And?'

'You would have liked it. It was a prime example of apartheid gothic and it proved Gerald's point three times over. You never know what's going on behind closed doors.'

I kept Dr Pinheiro and the letterbox museum to myself. At that time, I had spoken about them with no one but my mother and the secret had darkened into a superstition. At the heart of my memory something was in quarantine, for reasons I no longer remembered.

'The light failed, and you never took the photo; the light held, and you did. It seems so arbitrary.'

'I'm not too sure about that,' he answered. 'In a way it felt inevitable, as if I hardly had a choice. I was always drawn to the same things. I could pass by a corner twenty times and have the same thought: I've got to photograph this. Until I acted on that urge, it wouldn't let me go.'

'But can you square how the work is made and what it comes to stand for? There's such an air of necessity about your photos, as if it had to be these images and no others. It might look inevitable, read backwards, but it could all have been different. Every portrait could have been of someone else; every house could have been the house next door. If you'd turned down a different street, or passed by ten minutes later, or been less fond of driving.'

'I agree, a photograph is an odd little memorial that owes a lot to chance and intuition.' The espresso cup was like an eggshell in his fingers. 'But I was dogged, even if I say so myself. I used the available light. In the morning, I packed my camera bags and went out to take photographs, while more sensible men were building houses or balancing the books.'

Auerbach had an exhibition coming up. These days, he always had an exhibition coming up somewhere. 'I'm an artist, you know,' he joked, 'I can't help it. I've stopped arguing with the experts.' He spread some working prints out on the table like a deck of cards and we played rummy with them for a while.

I told him about the pictures I'd been taking. Even when he said, 'You should have brought them with you,' I did not mention the orange Agfa box in the boot of my car.

We spoke about my father and my uncle Doug, but what gripped me was the story about his friend Matti. They had known one another for years. The Finn had started coming to South Africa in the '70s, he said, covering the political situation for the European papers, and was glad of a place to stay when he passed through Johannesburg.

'We got on famously,' Auerbach said, 'although our approaches to photography could not have been more different. He should have been banging around in the war zones, but he didn't have the nerve. More gung than ho. South Africa was a good compromise. Once, just before he was due to fly back to Helsinki, he asked me if he could leave some clothing behind for safe keeping. His suitcase was open on the bed in the guest room – and it was full of film! Full to the brim with hundreds of spools. It looked like a conceptual artwork. It wouldn't be so strange today, now that every camera has a trunkful of film in it. Bytes weigh nothing and you don't pay for the excess. But I was shocked.'

The story reassured me enough to admit that I'd brought a few of my own photos with me. I fetched them and he gave them his attention. He was kind. He asked me questions and gave me pointers. It was more than the photos warranted.

Then, as I was getting ready to go, he said, 'You'll be interested in this.' He took a print from a folder and pushed it across the table. 'It's Joel Setshedi.'

A serious young man in a collar and tie, perched on the end of a desk in a panelled office. He is holding a framed photograph of himself, and in this one he is smiling broadly.

'The smaller photograph is Amos,' Auerbach went on, 'the twin brother. It's the portrait that stood on his coffin at his funeral. He died a couple of years ago, of Aids I suspect, although no one will say so. Joel keeps the picture on his desk. He works for a bank, the same one that employed his father, except he's in foreign exchange whereas the old man drove a delivery bike. He's done bloody well for himself, if you think where he started out, and he has his mother to thank. Veronica's still alive, by the way, retired to the family home in Limpopo. I'm going to photograph her too one of these days.'

Later, I went over this conversation in my mind and tried to name the aftertaste of envy in my admiration for Auerbach. He had a body of work and it held him steady in the world. More precisely: he *was* a body of work. A solid line. I had wasted my energies on trifles. Layered on one another, they created the illusion of depth, but it was never more than an effect. Most of all, I envied him his continuity. He had soldiered on, one photograph at a time, leaving behind an account of himself and his place in which one thing followed another, print after print. My own story was full of holes.

•

Janie wrote again re dead letters: 'It's a double whammy, isn't it? You want people to think you're making up the letters, because the story that they were left to you is so unlikely, but actually it's true. Fact is stranger than fiction, especially in novels. Your secret is safe with me.'

'Never should have told her,' Leora said.

'I know.'

'How did you respond?'

'I haven't written back, I don't want to encourage her. Next thing she'll ask me to be her friend on Facebook.'

'So?'

'It makes me think of lonely children with imaginary friends.'

'You should talk.'

There was a postscript to the email. 'You've got some dodgy role models. Koestler was a real bastard in his relationships with women. And that Eich character you're fond of quoting was a bit of a Nazi – if one can do such a thing by halves.'

And then a pps, fyi: 'Still working on your profile. Should be done in a week or two. Let me know what you think.'

It was Wellness Week at the mall. All along the high street, shops had set out tables laden with products for a healthier lifestyle. At the sportswear outlets, lithe young people in bodysuits were spinning, orbiting and rowing. The pharmacies displayed their ranges of vitamins and food supplements, alongside shower attachments, health sandals and bathrobes.

My eyes began to itch.

In the empty space at the bottom of the escalators, Miranda's Day Spa and Fitness World was offering free back rubs and foot massages to weary shoppers. People reclined in chairs with their pants rolled to their knees and their bare feet on footstools draped with plush white towels. Every single one of the acolytes kneeling before the stools to apply the aromatic oils was young, slim and beautiful, I noticed, while all the shoppers were old, fat and ugly. They must have followed their bliss into the nearest Wimpy once too often. One of the shoppers was talking into a cellphone pinned to her ear by a hunched shoulder, but most lay back with their eyes closed, their faces rapt, ready for whatever was on offer, oral sex or a sacrament. I remembered the photograph of Adriaan Vlok, the former Minister of Law and Order, kneeling to wash the feet of Reverend Frank Chikane, the former activist whom he had tried to poison, seeking a biblical absolution for the crimes of apartheid. I noticed the shoes abandoned beside the chairs, high heels that were bashfully pigeon-toed, trainers with their tongues hanging out. I remembered that there was no photograph of Adriaan Vlok and Frank Chikane: the story had simply been reported in the press.

The laying on of hands. It should be the other way round! The shoppers should be massaging the feet of the acolytes, doing penance for their gluttony, vanity and sloth.

Sucking in my belly, I went on. The outdoor-living shop had pitched a tent near their door and scattered some cotton-wool snow. There were racks of fleece-lined jackets, windcheaters and thermal vests, and tables full of equipment for extreme sports, adventure tourism, urban exploration and rural survival, like deodorized socks and rubber shoes for wading through streams. For a moment, the long gleaming corridor lined with cosmetic counters and knick-knack booths gave me the impression that I was in duty free, waiting for a flight, and I was overcome by jet lag.

The massage chairs were in the Court of the Sun King, arranged on the many wavy arms of a sunburst in mosaic tiles. Not a minute too soon. Most inviting was a green-leather chair facing the corridor that led to Exit 3. Although there are no exits at the mall, to be honest, only entrances. You can cash up, they say, but you can never leave. I sank into the chair's soft and yielding embrace and shut my eyes.

The Eagles were touring again, I'd seen them on television. They still had their hair and their teeth, as far as I could tell, but they were having back trouble like the rest of us, they had to sit down through the whole concert. It didn't seem right.

A human presence fell over me as lightly as a shadow. When I opened my eyes a salesman stood there. He had a bit of beard on his chin like a strip of Velcro. 'Chronic medical conditions?' he asked.

I stalled for a moment. Should I disclose my hypertension? Was it any of his business?

'Varicose veins, high blood pressure, fallen arches, slipped disks,' he prompted.

'No.'

'Taking any medication?'

This time I was ready: 'No.'

He threw the switch.

The chair stirred to life beneath me as if there was someone trapped in its spongy interior, someone trying to get out, I thought for a horrified moment, and then more worryingly, someone trying to pull me in. Kneecaps pressed into my legs, knuckles ground against my wrists. I was reminded of the playground and how children like to pummel one another, making their presence felt on one another's flesh. This is a mistake, I thought, I should get up now and go about my business. But the chair was an expert. It worked me over. The will in my muscles dissolved, the marrow of my resolve turned to water, the last hard fact was knocked out of me like a tooth. Whereupon the prisoner in the chair stopped struggling. The corridor stretched away into the distance like a canal. People were walking there on their reflections and I saw them waving as I sank.

•

Every day for a fortnight, I'd searched for my profile on Janie's blog. I learned to fold a dinner jacket so that it doesn't crease in a suitcase, to splint a broken arm with a rolled newspaper and keep aphids off rosebushes without using pesticides. No sign of me.

'For God's sake, *ask*,' Leora said. 'Give her a ring. Tell her the exhibition is coming up and she'd better get a move on.'

While I was still weighing the options, my mother left a message on my cellphone to say she'd seen the article in the *News*. My son the artist! Why didn't you tell me? She'd taken the paper to her bridge game and everyone agreed it made me seem very clever.

I was in the middle of a job, so I called Leora at home. She'd missed the piece too – who has time to read anything properly? – but she fetched yesterday's *News* off the stack under the sink and skimmed through it for me.

'It's like a bit of experimental fiction,' she said. 'It's in a dozen pieces with headings like "Motion Pictures" and "Stills" and there's a quote from some Frenchman and a paragraph in italics. She says you're a man of your time: disaffected without being disengaged. That part's in red. Do you get it?'

Yes. History has played a flame over me. I've come unstuck, but I'm joined to the world by a few gluey strands of saliva.

'There's a lot more,' Leora said. 'I'll put it aside and you can read it this evening.'

I had already decided not to. 'Just one other thing and then I'll let you go: what does she say about the photographs?'

When I was a boy, my father invented a game for us to play in the car. Perhaps it was a way to amuse an easily bored only child or a ruse to get an overtired one to fall asleep. I had to lie down on the broad back seat of the Merc, so that I couldn't see the road ahead, and when we came to the end of the trip I had to guess where we were. Looking up, my view hemmed in by door pillars and bulging seat-backs, I saw streetlights and treetops, sometimes a robot or the roof of a building, coming and going in the windows. Using only these lofty clues, I tried to keep track of our route. Sometimes I already knew our final destination, which made it easier, as my dad might stray from the main roads to fool me but was unlikely to go in a completely different direction. Just as often I had no idea where we were going. My father, for his part, looked for short cuts and detours. If my mother was with us, it was her job to see that I didn't sneak a look over the horizon of the window ledge, although I was seldom tempted. I loved the challenge. As we drove towards some familiar place, like Rosenthal's where my father bought his golfing gear or my grandparents' house in Orange Grove, I had to set what I remembered of the route we usually took against the stops and turns of the car, making rather than following a map and matching it not to the world but to an internal landscape, a journey in memory, keeping it clear until he pulled up and said, 'Okay, that's enough. Where are we?'

In the beginning, he always bamboozled me. All it took was one unexpected turn down a street we normally drove past and he could throw me off the trail. Then with every subsequent stop or bend in the road, the map I was making in my mind grew less and less reliable. If I was lucky, some landmark like the turnip-top of a water tower or the pylon lights at a sports stadium would let me pick up the thread, but often it was lost for good. Finally, my father would pull over and ask me the all-important question. After I had given my answer, I would sit up, and then we laughed to see how wrong I was. Once, after we had dropped some letters in the box at the post office, he drove us in a circle, so that when I thought we were close to home, it turned out we were back where we started. And once or twice, with the car rocking like a river barge on its soft suspension, I did in fact fall asleep.

As time went by and I discovered more subtle clues than those unreeling like a strip of film through the frames of the windows, I got better at the game and started to win sometimes. I learned to read the bumps in the road, the rumble of tar under the wheels, the way the car jolted across railway lines or yawed through subways. At night, colours fell through the windows from neon lights and robots, the sky was dark and smoky over Alex, and near the garages along Louis Botha Avenue the air smelt of rubber. My father had to work harder to mislead me. He varied his speed so that I lost a sense of distance, and circled around blocks so that I lost direction. He became as involved in the game as I was and liked to lose as little. A few times we dallied so long my mother thought something had happened to us, and when we got home, in high spirits from the fun, she ticked me off for making my father play silly games, when he was the one who had started it all.

A day came when I could not go wrong. It was a Friday evening. We had dropped Paulina at her bus stop, as she was going home for the weekend, and on the way back we stopped at a new fish-and-chip shop for takeaways. Usually my father would have been in a hurry to get home before the smell of the food got into the upholstery, but the unfamiliar territory drew us both into a game. I scrambled over the seat and stretched out in the back. We went down Louis Botha. Certainty settled over me like a blanket. I knew exactly where we were going. I had X-ray vision, I could see through the leather seats, where springs were coiled in fibre, I could see through the metal ribs of the door. Factory yards, shopfronts, garden fences and houses drifted by. My father turned off the main road earlier than he should have and wound through the crooked streets of Savoy. I saw the yellow-brick chimneys of the houses, the cars parked in driveways, the lights burning in windows. I had become a compass needle. Rather than trying to figure out where he was going, I was giving him directions, telling him when to slow down, where to turn, when to double back.

At last we stopped. The air was thick with the homely smell of food, which the vinegar had not entirely soured. I could see a streetlight on a tall pole, the jigsaw undersides of oak leaves, pieces of sky between branches. My dad's voice reached me through the wall of the seat: 'Where are we now, my boy?'

For the moment, I could not answer. I lay in the dark with the bitter knowledge that I had unlearned the art of getting lost.

Dear readers,

We rely on subscriptions from people like you to tell these other stories – the types of stories most UK publishers would consider too risky to take on.

Our subscribers don't just make the books physically happen. They also help us approach booksellers, because we can demonstrate that our books already have readers and fans. And they give us the security to publish in line with our values, which are collaborative, imaginative and 'shamelessly literary' (the *Guardian*).

All of our subscribers:

- receive a first edition copy of every new book we publish
- are thanked by name in the books
- are warmly invited to contribute to our plans and choice of future books

BECOME A SUBSCRIBER, OR GIVE A SUBSCRIPTION TO A FRIEND

Visit andotherstories.org/subscribe to become part of an alternative approach to publishing.

Subscriptions are:

£20 for two books per year

£35 for four books per year

£50 for six books per year

The subscription includes postage to Europe, the US and Canada. If you're based anywhere else, we'll charge for postage separately.

OTHER WAYS TO GET INVOLVED

If you'd like to know about upcoming events and reading groups (our foreign-language reading groups help us choose books to publish, for example) you can:

- join the mailing list at: andotherstories.org/join-us
- follow us on Twitter: @andothertweets
- join us on Facebook: And Other Stories

This book was made possible thanks to the support of:

Abigail Headon
Abigail Miller
Adam Biles
Adam Lenson
Adriana Maldonado
Ajay Sharma
Alan Bowden
Alan & Lynn
Alannah Hopkin
Alasdair Thomson
Alastair Gillespie
Alastair Kenny
Alec Begley
Alex Gregory
Alex Ramsey
Alex Read
Alex Sutcliffe
Alex Webber &
    Andy Weir
Alex H Wolf
Ali Smith
Ali Usman
Alison Anderson
Alison Bennets
Alison Hughes
Alison Layland
Allison Graham
Amelia Ashton
Amy Capelin
Amy Crofts
Ana Amália Alves

Andrea Reinacher
Andrew Marston
Andrew McCafferty
Andrew Nairn
Andrew Wilkinson
Angela Jane
    Mackworth-
    Young
Angus MacDonald
Ann McAllister
Anna Holmwood
Anna Milsom
Anna Vinegrad
Annabel Hagg
Anne Carus
Anne Meadows
Anne Withers
Anne Woodman
Anne Marie Jackson
Annette Morris &
    Jeff Dean
Annie Henriques
Anthony Messenger
Anthony Quinn
Archie Davies
Asher Norris
Averill Buchanan

Barbara Adair
Barbara Mellor
Barbara Zybutz

Bartolomiej Tyszka
Ben Coles
Ben Paynter
Ben Smith
Ben Thornton
Ben Ticehurst
Benjamin Judge
Bettina Debon
Bianca Jackson
Blanka Stoltz
Brenda Scott
Bruce Ackers
Bruce & Maggie
    Holmes

Camilla Cassidy
Candy Says Juju
    Sophie
Cara Eden
Cara & Bali Haque
Carole JS Russo
Caroline Rigby
Caroline Thompson
Carolyn A
    Schroeder
Carolyne Loosen
Carrie LaGree
Catherine
    Mansfield
Cecile Baudry
Cecily Maude

Celine McKillion
Charles Beckett
Charles Lambert
Charles Rowley
Charlotte Holtam
Charlotte Williams
Chris Day
Chris Gribble
Chris Stevenson
Chris Watson
Christina Baum
Christina Scholtz
Christine Luker
Christopher Allen
Christopher
   Marlow
Christopher Spray
Ciara Greene
Ciara Ní Riain
Claire Brooksby
Claire Williams
Claire Williams
Clare Buckeridge
Clare Fisher
Clare Keates
Clarice
   Borges-Smith
Clifford Posner
Clive Bellingham
Clive Chapman
Colin Burrow
Collette Eales
Craig Barney

Daisy
   Meyland-Smith
Damien Tuffnell
Dan Powell
Daniel Carpenter
Daniel Hugill
Daniel Lipscombe
Daniel JF Quinn
Daniela Steierberg
Dave Lander
David Archer
David Breuer
David Davenport
David
   Hebblethwaite
David Hedges
David
   Johnson-Davies
David Kelly
David Wardrop
David & Ann Dean
Debbie Pinfold
Deborah Smith
Denis Stillewagt &
   Anca Fronescu
Duarte Nunes

E Jarnes
Eamonn Furey
Ebru & Jon
Ed Tallent
Eileen Buttle
EJ Baker

Elaine Rassaby
Eleanor Maier
Elizabeth Boyce &
   Simon Ellis
Elizabeth Cochrane
Elizabeth Draper
Ellie Michell
Els van der Vlist &
   Elise Rietveld
Emily Jeremiah
Emily Jones
Emily Rhodes
Emma Kenneally
Emma
   McLean-Riggs
Emma Timpany
Eric Langley
Evgenia Loginova

Federay Holmes
Fiona & Andrew
   Sutton
Frances Perston
Francesca Bray
Francis Taylor
Freddy Hamilton

Gale Pryor
Garry Wilson
Gary Debus
Gavin Madeley
Gawain Espley
Gemma Tipton

Geoff Egerton
Geoff Thrower
George Sandison &
    Daniela Laterza
George Wilkinson
Geraldine Brodie
Gesine Treptow
Gill Boag-Munroe
Gillian Cameron
Gillian Doherty
Giselle Maynard
Gloria Sully
Glynis Ellis
Gordon Cameron
Gordon Campbell
Graham & Steph
    Parslow
Graham R Foster
Guy Haslam

Hannah Falvey
Hannah & Matt
    Perry
Harriet Gamper
Harriet Mossop
Harriet Sayer
Harrison Young
Helen Buck
Helen Collins
Helen Simmons
Helen Wormald
Helena Merriman
Helena Taylor

Helene Walters
Henrike
    Laehnemann
Howard Watson
Howdy Reisdorf

Ian Barnett
Ian Buchan
Ian Burgess
Ian Kirkwood
Ian McMillan
Imogen Forster
Inna Carson
Isabella Garment
Isfahan Henderson

J Collins
Jack Brown
Jackie Andrade
Jacqueline Haskell
Jacqueline
    Lademann
Jacqueline Taylor
James Barlow
James Cubbon
James Mutch
James Portlock
Jane Brandon
Jane Woollard
Janet Packard
Janette Ryan
Jasmine Gideon
JC Sutcliffe

Jenifer Logie
Jennifer Higgins
Jennifer Hurstfield
Jenny Diski
Jenny Kosniowski
Jenny McPhee
Jenny Newton
Jess Wood
Jillian Jones
Jo Elvery
Jo Harding
Joanna Ellis
Joanne Hart
Jocelyn English
Joel Love
Johan Forsell
John Allison
John Conway
John Corrigan
John Gent
John Glahome
John Nicholson
John William
    Fallowfield
Jon Riches
Jon Lindsay Miles
Jonathan Ruppin
Jonathan Watkiss
Jorge Lopez de
    Luzuriaga
Joseph Cooney
Joy Tobler
Judy Kendall

Julia Humphreys

Julia
   Sandford-Cooke

Julian Duplain

Julian Lomas

Julie Gibson

Julie Van Pelt

Juliet Hillier

Juliet Swann

Juraj Janik

Justine Taylor

Kaitlin Olson

Karan Deep Singh

Kasia Boddy

Katarina Trodden

Kate Gardner

Kate Pullinger

Kate Wild

Katharine Robbins

Katherine El-Salahi

Kathryn Lewis

Katie Martin

Katie Prescott

Katie Smith

Keith Dunnett

Keith Underwood

Kevin Brockmeier

Kevin Murphy

Kevin Pino

KL Ee

Krystalli
   Glyniadakis

Lana Selby

Lander Hawes

Laura Bennett

Laura McGloughlin

Laura Solon

Lauren Hickey

Lauren Kassell

Leanne Bass

Lesley Lawn

Leslie Rose

Linda Harte

Lindsay Brammer

Lindsey Ford

Liz Ketch

Lizzi Wagner

Loretta Platts

Louisa Hare

Louise Bongiovanni

Louise Howarth

Louise Rogers

Lyndsey Cockwell

Lynn Martin

M Manfre

Maggie Peel

Maisie & Nick
   Carter

Malcolm Bourne

Malcolm Cotton

Mandy Boles

Mansur Quraishi

Marella
   Oppenheim

Marese Cooney

Margaret E Briggs

Maria Potter

Maria Elisa
   Moorwood

Marieke Vollering

Marina Castledine

Marion Macnair

Marion Tricoire

Mark Ainsbury

Mark Blacklock

Mark Richards

Mark Waters

Mark T Linn

Martha Nicholson

Martin Conneely

Martin Hollywood

Martin Whelton

Martin Cromie

Mary Bryan

Mary Morris

Mary Nash

Mary Wang

Mathias Enard

Matthew Francis

Matthew Shenton

Maureen Cooper

Maxime
   Dargaud-Fons

Melanie Stacey

Michael Harrison

Michael Johnston

Michael Kitto

Michael Thompson
Michael &
    Christine
    Thompson
Michelle Purnell
Michelle Roberts
Minna Daum
Mirra Addenbrooke
Monika Olsen
Moshi Moshi
    Records
Murali Menon

Nadine El-Hadi
Nan Haberman
Nancy Scott
Naomi Frisby
Nasser Hashmi
Natalie Smith
Natalie Wardle
Nichola Smalley
Nicholas Holmes
Nick Chapman
Nick Sidwell
Nicola Hart
Nicola Hughes
Nikki Dudley
Nina Alexandersen
Nina Power

Olga Zilberbourg
Omid Bagherli

Paddy Maynes
Paola Ruocco
Pat Henwood
Patricia Appleyard
Patricia Hill
Patricia Melo
Paul Bailey
Paul Brand
Paul Dettman
Paul Gamble
Paul Jones
Paulo Santos Pinto
Pete Ayrton
Peter Burns
Peter Lawton
Peter Murray
Peter Rowland
Peter Vos
Phil Morgan
Phyllis Reeve
Piet Van Bockstal
Polly McLean
Pria Doogan

Rachel Kennedy
Rachel Parkin
Rachel Pritchard
Rachel Sandwell
Rachel Van Riel
Rachel Watkins
Read MAW Books
Rebecca Atkinson
Rebecca Moss

Rebecca Rosenthal
Regina Liebl
Réjane Collard
Renata Larkin
Rhodri Jones
Richard Carter &
    Rachel Guilbert
Richard Ellis
Richard Martin
Richard Smith
Richard Soundy
Rob
    Jefferson-Brown
Robert Gillett
Robert & Elaine
    Barbour
Robin Patterson
Ronnie Troughton
Ros Schwartz
Rose Cole
Rosie Hedger
Ross Macpherson
Ruth Clarke
Ruth Stokes

SA Harwood
Sabine Griffiths
Sally Baker
Sam Byers
Sam Gallivan
Sam Ruddock
Samantha Schnee
Sandie Guine

Sandra Hall
Sarah Bourne
Sarah Butler
Sarah Magill
Sarah Salmon
Sarah Salway
Sarojini
    Arinayagam
Sascha Feuchert
Saskia Restorick
Scott Morris
Sean Malone
Sean McGivern
Seini O'Connor
Selin Kocagoz
Sharon Evans
Sheridan Marshall
Sherine El-Sayed
Sian Christina
Sigrun Hodne
Simon Armstrong
Simon Blake
Simon Okotie
Simon Pare
Simon Petherick
Simon M Robertson
Sophie Johnstone
Stephen Abbott
Stephen Bass
Stephen Pearsall
Steven Williams
Stewart McAbney
Sue & Ed Aldred

Susan Bird
Susan Ferguson
Susan Hind
Susan Murray
Susan Tomaselli
Susan Wicks
Susanna Jones
Susie Nicklin
Suzanne Fortey
Sylvie Zannier-Betts

Tania Hershman
The Mighty Douche
    Softball Team
Thees Spreckelsen
Thomas Bell
Thomas Bourke
Thomas Fritz
Tim Russ
Tim Theroux
Tina Rotherham-
    Winqvist
Toby Aisbitt
Tom Bowden
Tony Crofts
Tony & Joy
    Molyneaux
Trish Hollywood

Vanessa Garden
Vanessa Nolan
Victoria Adams
Victoria O'Neill

Vinita Joseph
Vivien
    Doornekamp-
    Glass

Walter Prando
Wendy Knee
William Black
William Prior
William G Dennehy
Winifred June
    Craddock

Zoe Brasier

Current & Upcoming Books by And Other Stories

IVAN VLADISLAVIĆ was born in Pretoria in 1957 and lives in Johannesburg. His acclaimed fiction includes *Double Negative* (And Other Stories, 2013), *The Restless Supermarket* (And Other Stories, 2014), *101 Detectives* (And Other Stories, 2015) and *The Folly* (And Other Stories, 2015).

He has edited books on architecture and art, and sometimes works with artists and photographers. He has also written extensively about living in a changing South Africa. *Portrait with Keys* (Portobello Books, 2006) is a sequence of documentary texts about Johannesburg.

His work has won many awards, including the South African *Sunday Times* Fiction Prize, the Alan Paton Award for non-fiction and Yale University's Windham-Campbell Prize. He is a Distinguished Professor in Creative Writing at the University of the Witwatersrand.